S0-AIT-161

MAY – – 2023

CMPL
WITHDRAWN

GROUNDED

GROUNDED

A NOVEL

AISHA
SAEED

HUDA
AL-MARASHI

JAMILAH
THOMPKINS-
BIGELOW

S.K.
ALI

AMULET BOOKS · NEW YORK

CLINTON-MACOMB PUBLIC LIBRARY

PUBLISHER'S NOTE: This is a work of fiction. Names, characters, places, and incidents are either the product of the author's imagination or used fictitiously, and any resemblance to actual persons, living or dead, business establishments, events, or locales is entirely coincidental.

Cataloging-in-Publication Data has been applied for and may be obtained from the Library of Congress.

ISBN 978-1-4197-6175-1

Text © 2023 Aisha Saeed, Sajidah Kutty, Jamilah Thompkins-Bigelow, Huda Al-Marashi
Book design by Chelsea Hunter
Airport map by Natelle Qwek

Published in 2023 by Amulet Books, an imprint of ABRAMS. All rights reserved. No portion of this book may be reproduced, stored in a retrieval system, or transmitted in any form or by any means, mechanical, electronic, photocopying, recording, or otherwise, without written permission from the publisher.

Printed and bound in U.S.A.
10 9 8 7 6 5 4 3 2 1

Amulet Books are available at special discounts when purchased in quantity for premiums and promotions as well as fundraising or educational use. Special editions can also be created to specification. For details, contact specialsales@abramsbooks.com or the address below.

Amulet Books® is a registered trademark of Harry N. Abrams, Inc.

ABRAMS The Art of Books
195 Broadway, New York, NY 10007
abramsbooks.com

To our readers everywhere,
we hope you find what *you're* looking for

Zora Neale Hurston Airport

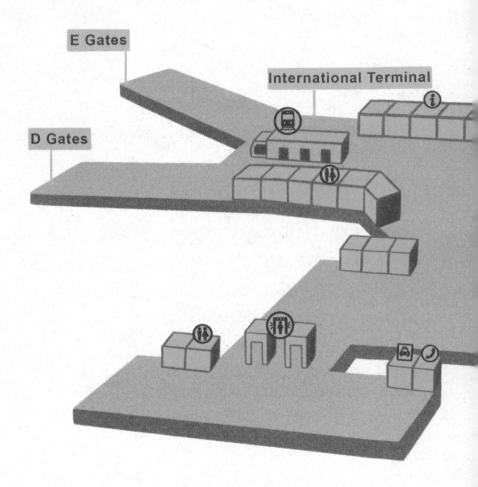

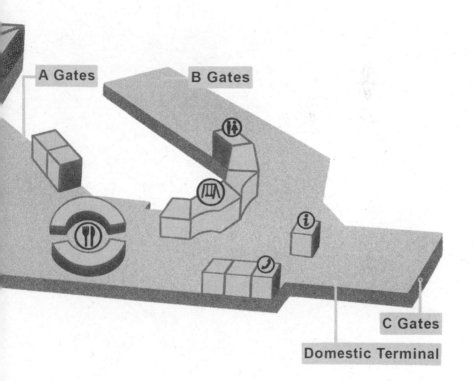

A Gates

B Gates

C Gates

Domestic Terminal

CHAPTER 1

FEEK

I'M GETTING TOO OLD FOR THIS STUFF. I MEAN, I'M TWELVE.
That's dumb close to teenager. Definitely too old to be spending
all my time with a four-year-old. A four-year-old sister named
Ruqi who talks too much and talks too loud, especially when I'm
trying to hear the rhymes in my head. Her voice jumps in front of
the lyrics every time.

Here in Hurston Airport's indoor playground, I'm watching
Ruqi *again* because my new baby brother, Hamza, started crying
again. Mom scooped him up and said she would be right back,
but I know that isn't happening. I look at my phone—7:33 P.M.
It's been ten minutes. Still no Mom.

Ruqi has lots to play with here: a fake helicopter with a slide,
a command center jungle gym, and the engine of a real airplane.
Even I would check out that engine if I was still a kid.

But Ruqi's not playing. She's skipping over to talk to me while
I'm watching *Storm the Stage,* a poetry slam show, on my phone.
It's hosted by Doc Hoffa, a rapper from way back who my parents
love. My family even got to visit his extra-lavish mansion with
marble and gold floors once, and that's one funny story—

"You not listening! Let's go on an adven-chuh!" Ruqi pulls my arm.

I shake her off and say, "The helicopter's an adventure. Look inside. See how far you can fly away." Thankfully, she hops over to it.

I'm chuckling, watching one poet describe himself as chocolate mousse, then cookie dough ice cream, when *it* happens: A rhyme drops into my mind.

I know from my dad, who performs poetry for a living, that when rhymes drop, you stop and catch them.

Because *it* doesn't just happen every day. Definitely not when I'm watching this show. On this show, these poets make me shut up and listen, make me suck in my breath, make me rip out pages from my rhyme book to start all over again. To try to be just as good.

But then, I freeze.

Can I write something that cool?

That question sucker punches my *it*.

Not this time. I'm thinking about the slick ways this poet is comparing himself to desserts. So smooth. But I would never describe myself that way, I think. Nah. I'm not sweets, I'm . . . And *it* drops:

I'm the words to the song
The hammer to the gong
The beats to this rhythm
The—

"FEEK!" Ruqi screams.

"What?! I'm writing! Go play!"

But as I try to get ahold of the rest of the words, she keeps yapping.

"Let's go to the shiny house! I wanna see it!" She's been calling the gigantic glass box thing near our gate "the shiny house" since we first passed it.

Focus, focus. What comes next? What rhymes with "rhythm"? But the words are gone.

And when I finally look up from my notebook, so is Ruqi.

But I didn't lose Ruqi. It's not like that. I bet she's at that glass thing she was talking about. I just got to be cool. Retrace our steps. Head back toward the gate.

I see that glass box with the silver tracks and metal balls inside that gleam even from a distance and almost run. Almost. I catch myself and remember the brand-new sneaks I'm wearing—white Air Force 1s that I finally convinced Mom to buy me. I'm not getting creases in them for nobody! Definitely not Ruqi. I speed-walk without bending my feet. It's kind of a waddle, but I do it smooth.

She's got to be there. It's surrounded by kids wearing kufis and khimars, which makes me smile as I pass my hand over my own kufi. There's hundreds of Muslims in this airport. Like us, everyone's leaving MONA, the Muslims of North America conference.

Inside that big glass box is a contraption of balls ping-ponging and spiraling around tracks and gears in chain reaction after chain reaction. It's kind of cool how they keep following the same maze-like path. I read the placard on the front: RUBE GOLDBERG MACHINE.

I almost reach out to pull the golden lever that activates the machine. I put my hands in my front hoodie pocket instead. A little boy pulls it, and five hanging steel balls start swinging back and forth. One ball hits the others. Clack! And the others hit back. Clack . . . clack, clack . . . clack, every ball has an impact. With all that going on, I see why little kids like Ruqi are into this thing.

But as I search the hijabbed heads around the machine, I don't see Ruqi's silver scarf with the sparkly unicorn headband she wears everywhere. I don't see Ruqi's face. My chest tightens. Is Ruqi okay? *Of course, she's okay! Breathe. Think . . . think . . .* Where would she go?

I feel a buzz in my pocket and check my texts.

Mom: Salaam. Sorry I'm taking so long. Hamza got poop everywhere. You two all right?

Where would Ruqi go?

Me: Yeah we're cool. I'm taking Ruqi to look at iPads.
Mom: Great. Meet me back at the gate when you're done.

Don't panic.

Mom: And sorry I exploded last night. Thanks for helping me so much with your sister.

I hear and feel a whimper come out of me when I think about last night. If Mom finds out I lost track of Ruqi again, I'll get a whole lot worse than yelling.

I shove my phone in my pocket. No way am I getting grounded. I didn't really lose her then, and she's not lost now. Not really. She's looking at iPads. She loves those. I flat-foot shuffle toward shops with flashy electronics that would grab a four-year-old. I stare hard into one store. *Please let Ruqi be here.* I can see from the startled eyes of a redheaded cashier with a tatted-up arm that I kind of spook her. I cock my head and give her my calmest, coolest smile. She smiles back. *Look calm*, I tell myself as I walk on. Looking calm makes things work out. Like last night.

At the fancy, boring conference banquet, listening to fancy, boring people speak, me and Mom and Hamza and Ruqi were sitting at a table with shiny dishes and too many forks and spoons for each person. As usual, Dad wasn't there. Dad is AbdusSalaam Stiles, or Salaam Stiles, as everyone calls him—the Muslim Lyricist. He had been performing nonstop at the conference and was sleeping in the hotel until his next performance later that night.

Hamza started crying at the table. Mom left with him. It was just me and Ruqi again, but at least she was being quiet.

While the fancy, boring speech droned on, rhymes filled my ears. I pushed aside my plate and plopped my notebook onto the table. I went in. I wanted Dad to see these new poems. To see how good I was getting. Almost as good as him. We could be a father-and-son team. I pictured him asking me to tour with him as "Feek Stiles, the Muslim MC." That made me laugh.

And then I was no longer hearing the fancy, boring speech. Instead, I heard Ruqi's voice—on full blast! I looked to the stage and blinked a few times at the light dancing off her headband. This had to be a bad dream. The keynote speaker was staring at Ruqi like they were sharing an inside joke, while Ruqi was holding the mic, telling the whole banquet why it was important to take turns letting people talk.

I waddle-ran up there and snatched the mic. *Look calm*, I told myself before telling the audience something I don't even remember that made them laugh, then yanking Ruqi off the stage. Mom yelled at me about it, said people came before poetry, family before art. But Dad's not here with us at the airport. So much for "family before art." I'm not mad about it. He has more important places to be than waiting around with us here.

I walk down the corridor. *Look calm, look calm, look calm . . .* Flat-foot step. A little smile. Ruqi isn't lost. She is fine. She has to be. I push away thoughts of anything bad happening to her and shuffle on until I almost trip on something shiny.

I look down and yelp. Ruqi's unicorn headband.

PEOPLE COME TO AIRPORTS TO CATCH FLIGHTS, TO GO PLACES.

But I'm here for another reason too.

I'm here for my number-one mission in life.

That's why I'm making my way back to TSA right now—far away from where Dad's waiting for our flight at gate B10. He doesn't know what I'm up to. He thinks we're just here to get on a plane to visit his cousin in New York before we fly home to Doha after the MONA conference. (But, of course, there are more important things in life. Like *life* itself.)

I notice an electronics store up ahead and slow down. Should I? Check how much Dad paid for the phone he bought me before the conference? (I just need to know if it's a bribe gift. Because.)

As I step inside the store, the phone in question reminds me not to get sidetracked from my mission by pinging a Google news alert for the keywords "Hurston airport cat missing."

FAMILY OF CAT MISSING AT HURSTON AIRPORT: IT'S BEEN A WEEK AND WE'RE HEARTBROKEN

I click and read the article, but there's no fresh information on Snickerdoodle, the cat.

Who is lost at this very airport I'm standing in right *now*.

A cat, scared for her life.

All alone, with no one to look out for her.

But not for long—because I'm going to find her!

As usual, I had been excited to come to the annual MONA conference. We'd been attending every summer since I was six, and now I have a crew of friends I meet up with each year, friends Dad finally let me hang out with by myself for the entire weekend. (While he did his own thing. A thing I knew about. That he didn't know I knew about.)

This year, the regular conference excitement had been multiplied by a thousand when I discovered that we were flying through *Zora Neale Hurston Airport*.

I'd be able to help find the lost Snickerdoodle.

It's my specialty.

Helping animals.

It's too bad my MONA friends are not here at the airport right now, though. They completely know me and get why I'm here on earth—for my life purpose—and would jump in to help me without missing a heartbeat.

I believe everyone has a life purpose and that this is mine: TO PROTECT AND SAVE ANY AND EVERY ANIMAL IN MY VICINITY BY ANY AND EVERY MEANS NECESSARY.

I also believe in Allah, and I think He put me here at this particular airport exactly a week after Snickerdoodle went missing for this reason: *I* had to be the one to reunite her with her heartbroken family. ("Heartbroken" has been mentioned in almost every article on Snickerdoodle. And, really, if any family *hadn't* been heartbroken about their cat wandering around pitifully in a huge airport, I'd probably want to give the lost animal to a better family.)

I found out about Snickerdoodle through the animal-rights forum I belong to, Animal Allies. We are a global forum of people of all ages who care about the well-being of *all beings*, not just humans. (That's the mission statement of AA. As soon as I read it, I clicked JOIN.)

I lean against a counter in the electronics store and open my notes app to reread the facts I've stored about Snickerdoodle.

Name: Snickerdoodle Mildred Hoffman
Age: Twelve
Hometown: Los Angeles, California
Went missing on: August 27
Where: TSA screening at Hurston Airport; escaped when pet carrier was opened during security examination
Answers to: "Snicker," "Doodles," and sometimes "Milly"
Likes: Meow Mix Treats, salmon flavor; nose strokes; shoes; lying on paper
Dislikes: Wide-open spaces, babies, vacuums, tall men

Where had I gathered this extra-special, extra-specific information from? That Animal Allies didn't provide?

Facebook. Which I'm not even allowed to join until I'm thirteen—not for another year and a half.

But *Dad* has a Facebook account, and before he banned me from it by changing his password, I used his account to message the Hoffman family on their page, SNICKERDOODLE IS MISSING: PLEASE HELP, to gather vital information. Like that Snickerdoodle loves Meow Mix salmon treats.

Which I have a huge pack of in my backpack now. To lure her when I find her.

I'd better head back to where she was last seen: the TSA security checkpoint. Dad wanted to go straight to our gate, so I wasn't able to take pictures of the scene of the crime when we passed through earlier. (It's a crime to lose an animal that was entrusted to the airport. In my mind it is, anyway. And if it isn't a crime in the airport's mind, I mean the airport staff's mind, then *that* is a crime too.)

Before leaving the electronics store, I quickly check the iPhones on display.

So Dad *had* spent a lot on my phone.

That makes me feel a tiny pinch of guilt.

I practically ignored Dad the entire weekend, answering in short one-word or few-words sentences to any question he'd asked.

And then I left him at gate B10 when he asked if he could talk to me about something "important."

I told him I needed to get food from the food court, which wasn't true *at all*. (I'd stuffed myself with pancakes at the all-you-can-eat, all-day breakfast restaurant before we got a cab to the airport.)

While Dad knew all about my interest in Snickerdoodle, he'd told me he didn't want me "wandering around the airport" so close to our departure time. Hence, the necessary secrecy.

Even though Dad is pretty laid-back at home with me, he's all about sticking to official rules about things in public, while I think not all rules are meant to be followed.

Like, if a pet has been missing for an *entire* week, and is dangerously close to *death*, it's time to break some rules.

Though I do feel a tiny bit sad remembering the way Dad's face and body slumped in the chair at the gate when I almost ran away from him.

But then I remember something else, and the sadness disappears. It's the thing I discovered when I used his Facebook account to message the heartbroken Hoffman family about Snickerdoodle.

Dad had signed up for the MONA matrimonial match dinner on Friday at the conference. And the MONA matrimonial speed match event on Saturday. And also the MONA matrimonial match database.

At first I didn't know what all that meant. But then I looked up "matrimonial" and learned it meant he wanted to get *married* again.

He'd been BUSY the entire weekend. Trying to get married.
BY ANY AND ALL MEANS NECESSARY.

Talk about having a life purpose. Mine is saving animals, and Dad's is getting a replacement mom for me? Without my permission?

I sigh heavily and then swallow a different sort of sadness clogging my throat before stepping out of the store.

I'm snapping some pictures of an empty corridor with carpeting (maybe very cozy for cats?) on my way to TSA when I see someone else, a kid my age, looking around for something. Could it be *another* lost pet?

I pause.

He's wearing a hoodie like mine, except his is white, while mine is teal and tied around my waist. His head is turning wildly around, peering into the corridor I'd just taken a pic of, then peering into the sunglasses kiosk opposite to it.

It's the kid who carried his little sister off the stage at the fancy MONA banquet dinner featuring Congresswoman Sarah Najjar.

He sees me looking at him and does a fast look away but then looks back and nods like he knows me or something.

It must be the MONA conference T-shirt I'm wearing.

"Did you lose something?" I ask. "A cat? Or some other pet?"

"What?" His body stills, and his hands go into his hoodie pockets. Like he's protecting himself. Or trying to look unfrantic. "Why?"

Yup, he's lost something. Something important.

"Because I'm looking for something too, and I can help you look?" I hold up my phone. "I'm looking for a lost cat myself. And I'm good at taking notes."

"You lost a cat here?"

"Not me." I swipe to find my screenshot of the SNICKER-DOODLE IS MISSING: PLEASE HELP Facebook page. "This family lost Snickerdoodle."

"You know them or something? The people who lost their cat?"

"I'm doing them a service," I say, wondering if I should say I'd been hired by the heartbroken Hoffmans—because they *had* communicated with me via Dad's Facebook messages. "I'm working for them. And I can help you too."

He looks at me like some people do when I go on about animals for too long: eyebrows scrunched, trying to figure out whether I'm too weird to talk to or some kind of cool they don't know yet. I swipe my phone again and show him my notes. I don't know if that's convincing, but he takes his hands out of his hoodie pockets and says, "Okay, yeah, I lost my sister."

Whoa.

CHAPTER 3

SAMI

PLEASE DOWNLOAD.

Please download.

Please download.

Turns out pleading with your iPad does not, in fact, make it work faster. I bite my lip—the flight-tracker app is refusing to load. Not that it's my iPad's fault. This airport is the worst! The longest security line, the most pointless food court (half the restaurants are closed and it's not even nine o'clock!), the most uncomfortable seats, and seriously the worst Wi-Fi in the history of humanity. I really wish I had a phone.

My parents and I are situated strategically by the boarding entrance, our backs to the floor-to-ceiling windows overlooking the planes coming and going. I can't stop myself from continuously peering back at the tarmac. Our flight takes off soon, but the plane is nowhere to be found.

"I have a bad feeling," I murmur.

"It'll be okay." My father ruffles my hair.

"And my iPad barely works," I complain. "There's a good app to track flights, but—"

"Patience, Sami. Following the plane's flight path won't make it come any sooner."

He's right. I know he's right. But—

"I'll just check the monitors," I tell my parents.

"Good idea." My mother nods. "And I'm sure the plane will be here before you know it."

I'm not so sure about that. I stick my tablet in my book bag and look at the gray clouds outside blotting out any stars or moonlight.

I carefully avoid outstretched legs and the luggage strewn in the aisles as I make my way toward the bright-blue electronic board listing departure times.

Stepping into the hallway, I nearly bump into a golden-brown retriever.

"Woof!" He's wagging his tail at me and wears a sign that reads TRAVEL BUDDY.

"Would you like to pet him?" the woman holding the leash asks.

"Uh—" I say.

"Sometimes animals like Biscuit here visit airports. They're ready to snuggle anyone who wants to feel a little better about their flight." She smiles. "Can be a little nerve-racking for some people sometimes."

Do I look *that* freaked out? Did this dog beeline straight for me?

I awkwardly pat the dog's head. "Uh. He's . . . cute. I have something I was on my way to do, but thanks."

I jostle for a spot among the other travelers crowded around the monitor and look up at the departure times. Finally, I see it. MCO. The three-letter code for Orlando, Florida. On time. Which should make me feel better, except I'm not so sure about that.

For one thing, we're supposedly boarding in thirty minutes, and our plane isn't even here yet. For another thing, those are some *super*-dark and low-hanging clouds gathering out the window behind where my parents are sitting. Cumulonimbus clouds are not something you want to see when you need your flight to take off as soon as possible so you can at least get *some* rest before your very first away karate competition.

Sensei Madea is counting on me. He said so himself. I'm the one who has the roundhouse kick down best. Last week at practice, we all had to show him our best moves, and I nearly toppled *him*!

"Way to go!" He grinned once he caught his balance. He gave me a huge high five. "You're going to help us bring home the championship, Sami!"

My outfit is pressed and starched and hanging behind my bedroom door. I even made a list of all sorts of fun stuff we can play as a group on the bus ride up like mafia, celebrity, and heads-up. (Coach Madea said we're *not* going to zone out on our phones for the whole drive, which works for me, since I don't *have* a phone.) And since the dojo's only two miles from the University of Florida, my big brother, Ibrahim, said he would come to cheer me on!

But if this flight doesn't take off as planned, everything will be ruined.

Ibrahim always tells me there's no point in worrying about things that are out of your control. Half the time, whatever you're freaking out about doesn't even happen.

Except that means that the other half of the time, it does.

And right now, I flinch as the blue "on time" departure next to Orlando switches to a bright red "delayed" and the time flips from 9:30 P.M. to 9:35 P.M.

It's just five minutes, I tell myself as my pulse quickens. *Three hundred seconds.* That's all. Except, actually, *no.* That's not all. I know how this goes. First it's five minutes. Then ten. Then thirty. Then . . .

No, no, no. I shake my head and take a step away from the monitors and try to channel my brother. Five minutes might really just be five minutes. Everything could be okay. But as much as I tell myself this, my hammering heart refuses to believe me.

"Ruqi! Where are you?" a boy shouts out.

A boy and a girl—both about my age—hurry in my direction.

"Stop playing!" he says. "This isn't funny!"

"Don't worry, Ruqi's around here somewhere," the girl reassures the boy.

The girl's hair is tied up in a ponytail, and she has on glasses. A colorful scarf is tied like a lasso around one of the loops of her jeans. The boy looks familiar. As I get closer, I take in his dark jeans and his shoes—the super-white Nikes—and I realize I definitely *did* see him.

He was at the conference, and his little sister jumped onto the stage during the final keynote address. She'd marched up to that microphone and spoken with so much confidence, her voice echoing through the room, that for a second I thought maybe *she* was the keynote speaker (even though her head didn't peek over the podium). The boy scooped her from the stage, but not before leaning in and joking about her being the warm-up act. Everyone laughed.

Some people really do stay cool, calm, and collected, even when their little sister leaps onto the stage. I could *never* have done that. Even the little girl, who couldn't have been more than five, was cooler than I could ever be. Although, as I see him closer up, he looks a little flustered right now.

When I check the monitor again, my heart drops straight to my feet. The time has changed again. Our flight is officially ten minutes late. And there is still no plane at the gate. I take a deep breath in and out. Again. And again. It doesn't help.

"Relax," Ibrahim would tell me if he was here right now. "Instead of fixating on what's freaking you out, do something to get your mind off things."

He's right. Freaking out just makes you freak out more—it's like a spiraling stack of dominoes crashing down. I know a ten-minute delay (for now!) isn't the end of the world. There are way worse things happening in the universe right this very minute. I just wish my brain could get through to my heart, which isn't listening at all. Beads of sweat pop up along my forehead.

As I approach the bathroom to splash my face with water, a boy stumbles out. He's the same kid from earlier. Up close, I can see he looks scared.

Maybe even more than me right now.

"Are you—are you okay?" I ask.

He looks at me and slowly shakes his head. "I—" he begins, but before he can finish his sentence, we hear a shout.

"Ruqi?" It's the girl with the lasso scarf. She's hurrying out of the girls' bathroom next door. Looking at the boy, she shakes her head. "Not in there either."

"We're running out of places," he says. There's a quiver in his voice.

"Don't worry," she says. "We'll find her."

The puzzle pieces start to come together. The girl from yesterday. She's missing. No wonder this boy looks terrified.

"Do you need help?" I ask. "Security's got a desk down the hall past my gate."

The girl looks at me with surprise. She brightens a little. Uh-oh.

"We *could* use some help." She nods. "I'm Hanna. This is Feek. His little sister, Ruqi, wandered off, and it's kind of an all-hands-on-deck situation. Maybe you could help us cover more area?"

They want *my* help? The kid who was on his way to douse his face in the sink to fend off a meltdown? I glance at Feek, but he's busy scanning the gate behind me.

"Oh. That's . . . that's awful," I say. I lost track of my parents at Disney World when I was five, and I still feel slightly trauma-tized. Ruqi must be terrified! But why are they looking for her themselves?

"I have a flight," I tell her. "But we should alert—"

"Yeah, we *all* have flights." She frowns.

"Sh-shouldn't we tell someone?" I try again. "Security? The police?"

"Security?" She crinkles her nose. "Security here is not exactly amazing—trust me on that. Feek's got some good ideas of where she's dashed off. We're narrowing it down by process of elimination."

"Yeah," Feek says. "She's gotta be here somewhere."

My cheeks flush. I'm nervous to say no. But I'm equally nervous to say yes. When I look at Feek and Hanna discussing the next place they'll search, I can see Feek's worry waft over him like swirls of frost.

They need help.

I think of Ibrahim: "Instead of fixating, do something."

I glance at the departure monitor. Sure enough, our delay has gone from ten minutes to thirty minutes. I join Feek and Hanna. We take off at a brisk pace down the hallway. I might not be able to control that departure board, but I can definitely do this. I can try to help them find Ruqi.

CHAPTER 4
NORA

THE CHOCOLATE GARDEN WAS CLOSED. C-L-O-S-E-D. DOORS locked, lights off, CLOSED.

It's my favorite place in the world, and my mom promised to take me for my "special" birthday trip this weekend. She was giving the keynote address at some Islamic convention, and she said it would be fun for us to have some quality time together.

So I spent DAYS planning my trip to the Chocolate Garden—my outfit and all the videos I was going to post on NokNok—because I'm a SWEETIE, which is kind of like a foodie, but I post about all things SWEET!

Me at French bakeries!

Me at old-fashioned ice cream parlors!

Me at fine candy stores!

And the Chocolate Garden *was* going to be me in chocolate heaven.

BUT my mom had appearances and meetings booked the entire weekend, and by the time we stopped at the Chocolate Garden on our way to the airport, the only thing left for me to do was look through the darkened windows.

Now I'm stuck at the gate with Congressmom, the super-important Sarah Najjar. She's taking a call, and I'm scrolling through NokNok and seriously wondering why she even had me. Like, should you be a parent if you can't provide for your kid's basic needs for chocolate and NokNok? (Which is my job, okay? It's not all fun. It's more like homework, and parents are supposed to help you with your homework.)

And yes, it is a NEED. Not just a want, like my mom was trying to convince me. She consoled me that there was another Chocolate Garden branch in the airport, but when we got here, it was CLOSED, too.

My mom doesn't understand that the Chocolate Garden's dreamy milk chocolate, nougat, and pretzel bar is seriously the best thing I've ever put in my mouth, and posting about it was going to boost my follower count. My two best friends, Kennedy and Mackenzie, eked past me with their hair tutorials just last week. Which really bothered me. Like there aren't already a million people doing hair on NokNok!

Thinking about all the ways my hopes have been dashed this weekend frustrates me so much that I grab my stuff and move four seats down.

As soon as I sit, I hear a notification on my phone.

Mackenzie: AAAH, how was it? Bet you got a ton of clips
Kennedy: What time is your birthday party when you get back? Can't wait

I stare at their messages, but I can't think of what to write back. We've been friends since the first grade, but sometimes they don't understand my life. They're always telling me how lucky I am because I go on all these trips with Congressmom, but they don't see this side—the canceled plans, the getting dragged to a Muslim conference where I felt totally out of place.

That last part I definitely don't discuss with my friends. My mom is always telling me how her grandparents came from Lebanon and how they worked hard to build a good life for their children and grandchildren. She wants me to grow up to be a strong Arab American, Muslim woman, but I don't feel Arab or Muslim. Going to MONA only made that feeling worse.

We don't practice Islam like the people at MONA, praying and fasting, eating halal meat. There's only one other Muslim kid in my class, a girl named Sumaya, and things are COMPLICATED between us.

I reread Kennedy and Mackenzie's messages. Do I tell them I didn't make it to the Chocolate Garden? How do I explain that?

I slide my phone into my purse. Maybe they'll think I'm already in the air.

Air is exactly what I need right now. But since I can't go outside, I'll settle for something sweet. I bet the only thing worth trying in the food court is a sad cinnamon roll from Cinna-Yum, the boring dessert you can find in any mall.

I sigh loudly, hoping Mom will hear me. The commonness of a cinnamon roll, after thinking about Crunchy Fluffy Dream Bars, is SO depressing.

Mom doesn't look over, so I walk back, tap her shoulder, and stick out my hand. She's still on her call, but she digs into her work bag and hands me a twenty-dollar bill before sending me off with an air kiss.

I head toward the food court with my carry-on bag. My first order of business is to put on the outfit I had planned to change into at the Chocolate Garden. I may find some interesting candy in a gift shop, and there's no way I'd go on camera in the outfit I'm wearing now. Mom packed me a separate wardrobe of "Muslim" clothes—long-sleeve button-up shirts and headscarves that I let fall onto my shoulders most of the time.

At every gate, I see Muslim families: moms in hijab, teenage daughters in hijab, some dads wearing caps. I recognize some of their faces after seeing them for two days straight.

One family in particular stands out. Their little girl climbed onstage before my mom's keynote and gave her own speech before her big brother dragged her away. I don't see the little girl and her brother now, but the mom is nursing the baby under her scarf. She gave those kids the sternest look when she came back to the table. I couldn't stop stealing glances at them all night.

Seeing these MONA families makes me want to change out of these clothes even faster.

When I finally step into the food court, in a super-cute knee-length turquoise summer dress with a subtle ruffle on the hem, I feel more like myself. I decide on a Cinna-Yum *and* a decaf iced mocha latte with whipped cream because I deserve it.

While I wait in line, I glance over at the Chocolate Garden, with its locked metal gate. Maybe I'll take a sad shot in front of the CLOSED sign to post later, after I come up with a good story about why we didn't make it there. Sad posts are great because people feel sorry for you.

When I turn back, I'm surprised to see the girl from my mom's speech at the front of the line. She's ordering something, but then a Cinna-Yum employee motions for her to follow him.

The name Ruqi comes to me. Her brother made a joke about how Ruqi was warming up the crowd. It was the funniest part of the weekend. Even my mom got a laugh when she said, "There goes my future intern."

But now Ruqi's alone. I hear the employee say, "Do you know where your mom is?"

Any other kid would have been scared, but she calmly replies, "I'm not supposed to bother her, but I want a Cinna-Yum."

Even though she says "supposed" like *deposed*, and "bother" like *bovver*, this is one confident preschooler. I didn't talk to anyone but my mom all weekend, and here goes Ruqi ordering by herself at Cinna-Yum—and, from the looks of it, without any money.

I look behind me and to either side. Her mom must still be feeding the baby, but her brother is probably going to show up any minute now and yank her away again.

I return to the menu. This kid is not my problem. My problem is the Chocolate Garden three stores down taunting me with its locked doors. I need to order my Cinna-Yum and iced mocha latte, maybe take my sad picture in front of the Chocolate Garden, and get back to my gate.

But for some reason, I can't stop turning around to see if the brother is coming.

The employee asks the cashier to call security, and that's when I feel terrible. If I don't say something, this is going to turn into a huge thing that is going to freak out this kid and her family.

Ugh. Am I really going to do this? I'm turning into Congressmom, sticking my nose into other people's business.

I step out of the line and walk over to Ruqi and the employee. "Wait," I say. "I can help find her family."

Ruqi looks up at me, puzzled, and I feel silly. Even though I recognize Ruqi from the speech, she doesn't know who I am.

I don't want the employee to think I'm a creepy kidnapper, so I crouch down until we're eye to eye and say, "Assalamu alaikum, Ruqi."

The words almost startle me. I've never used that greeting before, and I don't know how it got into my mouth. "I was at MONA too. I can take you back to your mom."

"But I want my Cinna-Yum," Ruqi says, completely unbothered.

I remember my twenty-dollar bill. There's plenty for the both of us.

"We'll take two Cinna-Yums," I say. I don't mention my drink. Something tells me I'm going to need two hands until I get this kid back to her family.

CHAPTER 5

FEEK

I'M GRIPPING THE UNICORN HEADBAND IN MY HOODIE POCKET.
I'm holding it to keep my hands from doing what every instinct
is telling me to do, which is to grab my phone and call Mom
right now. To tell her I messed up. To cry like a baby. To say, "I
don't know where Ruqi is, she wasn't at the machine thing, she
wasn't with the iPads, she wasn't in the bathroom, and she left her
goofy headband even though she wears it to bed, and a horrible
person has probably run away with her or maybe she got stuck on
a conveyor belt and has gone wherever all lost luggage goes, and
now we'll never see her again!"

I squeeze the headband and take a deep breath. I can't tell
her that.

Stay cool. Hanna seems to know what she's doing. With the
way she's typing so much into her notes app, she's got to know
something.

But what if the scared-looking boy who's walking with us was
right? Maybe we do need security. I look back at him and take in

his light-blue polo tucked into jeans I'd never wear. The kind worn by kids who run and tell teachers everything—even stuff that isn't that bad—and get everyone in trouble. Nah.

I turn to Hanna. "Where should we go now?"

Tucked-in shirt says, "Does Ruqi like stuffed animals? I think I saw a gift shop back—"

"No, that wouldn't be right." Hanna holds up her hand. "When cats go missing from their families for too long, they lose their zest for play. They seek their most basic needs for survival: food and shelter. Ruqi must be in search of a food source."

I fix my face to not show how confused I am by her professional language. It's been only thirty minutes. Is Ruqi already starving? And is she calling my sister a cat?

"So . . . the food court?" I ask.

"Yes, let's go immediately," Hanna says.

"Cool." I sigh, and then the whimpered question is out of my mouth before I have time to stop it: "What if she isn't there either?"

"We have to make dua that she is," Hanna says. In one fluid motion, she whips a scarf out of her belt strap and slings it around her head. Who is this girl?

She cups her hands. "Say it with me: Inna lillahi wa inna ilaihi raji'un."

I gasp. "The dua we say when someone dies?"

Tucked-in shirt's brown face turns almost white.

"You can also say it when you lose something," Hanna explains. "Now pray."

I slowly exhale. Ruqi is okay. This is a prayer for when someone is lost too.

We bow our heads and say it together, "Inna lillahi wa inna ilaihi raji'un."

As we enter the busy food court, I think about that prayer: from God we come. *Ya Allah, let Ruqi come!* And I tell myself to believe it. Ruqi will come. In the way Hanna almost marches into the food court, I see that Hanna believes it too. Ruqi will come. Even tucked-in shirt is with us, though he trails behind, his eyes darting everywhere like he's scared. I slow my breathing and my walk. My grip on the headband loosens. *Look calm. Be calm. Ruqi will come.*

And then, can you believe it? Ruqi is standing outside Cinna-Yum with a cinnamon roll and laughing like everything's fine! I almost run to pull her into a hug, but then I realize:

Ruqi's just standing outside Cinna-Yum with a cinnamon roll and laughing like everything's fine.

Like I wasn't just begging Allah to save her from a kidnapper named Brutus. Like I wasn't just thinking about all the ways a kid could get trapped or worse in an airport.

I march up to her and call her by her full name the way Mom does when she's mad at us. "Ruqayyah Khalilah Stiles! Where have you been?"

"Feek!" She even has the nerve to smile. "This is Nora! My fwiend!"

"Don't you 'Feek' me! I've been looking everywhere for you. I even had to get people to help, Hanna and, and, and—"

"Sami," the boy says quietly.

"Right, Sami! You got me, Hanna, and Sami running all over this airport for you because you want to get a snack! When are you gonna grow up?"

Ruqi's eyes are wide now. Good, she needs to know how serious this is.

"And you even left your headband!" I say, pulling it out of my pocket.

Her mouth forms an O as she pats her head, feeling that it's gone.

She reaches for her headband, but I snatch my hand away. I feel a weight lift off my shoulders as I let loose on her. "I am too old to keep playing these games! It's bad enough I have to spend all my time babysitting you, but then you run off too!"

"It's not her fault," some girl says. I look behind Ruqi and notice the girl, her arms folded and her face red with anger. Ruqi pulls the headband out of my hand.

OF COURSE *NOW* THE BROTHER AND TWO OTHER MONA KIDS show up as Ruqi and I are about to leave. Where were they before I bought Ruqi a Cinna-Yum and gave up on my iced mocha latte?

My hands go straight to my hips, and my face grows hot. The brother—I guess his name is Feek—jumps into lecturing Ruqi. You can tell he's one of those kids who thinks he's older than he is, wearing one of those Muslim hats and brand-new Nike Air Force 1s. At least the two other kids he's with look appropriately freaked out. As freaked out as Ruqi's brother should be! The girl, Hanna, I recognize from MONA because she always had a pack of friends in matching T-shirts with her. This poor Sami kid I don't recognize. His clothes have more of a *blending-in* kind of style.

I'm about to interrupt and say, "Hey, I found your sister trying to order this Cinna-Yum that I actually bought for her," because I can't deal with this Feek kid's responsible-older-brother act. But I worry it will sound petty to be talking about who bought whom a Cinna-Yum.

Instead, I say, "It's not her fault. She's little, and this is not the first time you lost her."

Feek, Hanna, and Sami look me up and down. They're

surprised I know about Ruqi climbing onstage. They must have seen my outfit and assumed I wasn't at MONA.

It annoys me that they're judging me by my clothes, even though I guess I do it too. Sometimes Kennedy, Mackenzie, and I talk about what people are wearing and what we would do to make their outfits better. Lately I've been trying to keep my comments about only style and not judging people. Still, this whole weekend, I couldn't stop thinking about what Kennedy or Mackenzie would say if they saw me at MONA, and now I've got these guys who can't believe I was at MONA either.

Feek says, "Wait a minute. What do you mean, this isn't the first time I lost her?"

I roll my eyes. Does he always have to play things cool?

"Because it was my mom's speech Ruqi interrupted," I say, and a flash of embarrassment passes over his face.

Hanna, however, looks starstruck. A lot of people make that expression when I tell them who my mom is, and I'm not gonna lie, there are times when dropping that piece of information is very helpful.

"Congresswoman Najjar is your *mom*?" Hanna asks.

Now that I have the upper hand in this conversation, I lock eyes with Feek and add, "Yup. That's how I recognized Ruqi. So I offered to bring her back to your family before the Cinna-Yum people called security and this turned into a huge deal for you."

Feek doesn't acknowledge that I saved him. Instead, he says, "Hey, I was about to find her myself. Hanna here is a professional."

Just when I thought these kids could not get any weirder. How can an eleven-year-old be a "professional"? Now I really NEED to put this whole weekend behind me, but first I say, "Whether you were about to find her or not, the nice thing to say to the person who *did* find her is thanks."

I grab my roller bag and my Cinna-Yum, and I'm about to make a dramatic exit when Hanna grabs my arm and says, "Wait! Don't leave! I desperately need your help!"

I WONDER IF I SHOULD STAND ON A CHAIR. TO GET THEIR focused attention. Especially the girl in the dress who says she's Congresswoman Sarah Najjar's daughter.

A congresswoman getting involved with Snickerdoodle's rescue would be *so* important to Animal Allies.

Maybe we can finally get action.

Congresswoman Najjar can write a law that says traveling animals must have a separate part of the airport to prepare for their flights so they don't get lost. Like a special, exclusive lounge. Maybe called *Cubhouse* or *Pup-park* or something.

She could even make all airlines have a pet section on their planes, one that's not in the cargo. (BECAUSE LIVING BEINGS ARE NOT LUGGAGE.)

I start to climb the chair but then catch Feek's eyes. He looks at me like he's worried about what I'm going to do. From my estimation, Feek is the type who wouldn't want the entire food court paying attention to us.

He's my client, and I like clients, so I decide to kneel on the chair instead.

"Ruqi is safe now. But . . . *is Snickerdoodle?*" I pause for dramatic effect. Sarah Najjar's daughter must be used to hearing a lot of speeches, and I want mine to get her attention. And then she can help me get her mom's attention.

But the daughter just grabs the handle of her carry-on like she's going to storm off.

"WAIT!" I say again, reaching out so abruptly I almost fall out of the chair, my headscarf falling forward and then back off my head to settle around my neck. I talk fast. "There's a missing cat at this airport! She's been missing for a week! Her name is Snickerdoodle! She may have been seen a couple of days ago! She's hiding somewhere, all scared! She needs to be rescued! Her family is heartbroken, so heartbroken! A million times heartbroken! WE NEED TO FIND HER!"

Everyone—Feek, Sami, Ruqi, the congresswoman's daughter—stares at me.

So, for speeches, maybe speed-talking works?

I pull off my scarf, wind it back through my belt loop, and knot it swiftly. Then I take off my backpack. Unzipping it, I grab the five hundred grams of salmon-flavored Meow Mix and hold it up before sticking my hand back in the bag for the only other visual I need: a printout of Snickerdoodle herself.

Real pictures are better than digital ones.

You can see the sad eyes more clearly.

I unfold the paper and thrust the image of the Himalayan cat into the other kids' faces, banking on them falling hard for the fluffy, dusty-white, long-haired cuteness. (Though she *does* have a smudgy-gray Himalayan cat face some people think looks real grumpy. I hope these guys don't think she looks real grumpy.)

"I've been working on this case on my own. But now I can use all your help! Let's go find Snickerdoodle!"

"You're stalking a cat?" Sarah Najjar's daughter crosses her arms.

Sami's eyes are darting around like he needs to find the bathroom. Or like he's embarrassed.

Or like he's trying to understand the case?

"Cookie Cat!" Little Ruqi grabs the paper from my hand so abruptly that it rips and I'm left holding Snickerdoodle's droopy eyes and the part that says, LOST CAT AT THE AIRPORT.

Oh no . . . it was my only picture of her. How am I going to get more people invested in the mission now?

"We've got some time before we board, so yeah, me and Ruqi can help," Feek says. "You helped me find Ruqi. So yeah, for sure."

A client testimonial.

I turn to him, grateful. Maybe I can get him to sign up for Animal Allies too. "Snickerdoodle and hundreds of traveling animals like her are thanking you right now, Feek. You may not be able to hear them, but they are sending you silent messages of gratitude." This time, I don't pause for effect but whip my head to the others. "Who else is in?"

I stare at Sami first, afraid to turn with appealing eyes to the most important asset: Congresswoman Najjar's daughter.

If Sami is in, maybe she'll be too?

CHAPTER 8

SAMI

WHAT. IS. HAPPENING?

Snickerdoodle?

Don't get me wrong. I feel horrible for this poor animal, but that doesn't change the fact that rescuing an animal is one million miles outside my range of expertise. Not to mention that it's—I check the wall clock—8:24 P.M., and I have a flight I need to hurry back to my gate to catch.

Hanna glances at me expectantly for a split second (at which point my brain goes blank) before she moves on to pleading her case with the girl who found Ruqi. And Hanna is on a roll. I wait for a pause in the monologue so I can politely let her and Feek know I'm relieved Ruqi is safe, and while I *really* am rooting for Snickerdoodle, I've got to get going. But Hanna waves her phone, explaining the situation a mile a minute, which makes it hard to figure out how to get myself out of this politely.

Nora's hands are on her hips. She looks at Hanna with an expression I recognize because it's one I've seen thrown my way by people in school countless times. The "are you kidding me what is seriously wrong with you" look.

It happened just last week. That look. The Bunsen burner was about to *boil over*, so I waved my hands frantically for my teacher to come make sure there wasn't some sort of environmental hazard about to unfold. (It was really hot!) Turns out I'd just put in too much baking soda.

"Scaredy-cat Sami strikes again." Jackson smirked from the next table as all the boys sitting there erupted into laughter.

Looking at Nora, she's shooting the same kind of look. But unlike me, who takes that kind of look as my cue to scurry away, Hanna either doesn't notice or doesn't care. Both of which are pretty impressive, because Nora is getting more and more visibly irritated with each passing second.

I glance back in the direction of my gate. Uh-oh. It's not even visible from where I'm standing. My parents have no idea where I am. I pull out my tablet from my book bag, and that confirms it. No signal. They could be FaceTiming me over and over, and I wouldn't even know it! Ruqi Part Two, the Sami Edition, could be taking place at this very moment. And even if somehow they're completely chill about my being missing for the last ten minutes, the flight might be boarding. It's time to go. And if we're being honest, it's not like Hanna needs my help. Before I can say anything, Nora holds up her hand.

"Look," Nora says as Hanna launches into her top three theories. "It sounds like there's actual experts helping with this cat thing. And from everything you've said, they're doing all they can."

Yes, Nora! I silently cheer. She's saying exactly what I've been trying to get through to Hanna since we met. Let experts handle situations requiring expert help!

"Exactly!" Hanna says, undeterred. "They're doing everything they can, but *it hasn't worked.*"

"And *you're* going to figure it out?" Nora retorts. "What are you, like, ten?"

"Eleven and a half. But that doesn't matter. I know what I'm talking about here." She says it confidently, but I see pink rising on her cheeks. So she does care, at least a little bit. I agree with Nora, but she didn't have to say it like *that.*

"You don't have to be so harsh. Hanna's a pro," Feek says quickly.

Hanna smiles. "Thanks, Feek."

"I wanna help too!" Ruqi squeals.

"Sounds like you've got yourself a team," Nora says dryly. "Good luck."

I watch Nora walk away. Great. Now seems like the worst time to let Hanna know I have to go too. I clear my throat. I'll assure Hanna I'm *not* leaving because I don't believe in her. It's that I believe in her so much I know she doesn't need me. I brighten. Yes, that's it.

But before I can say anything, a bolt of lightning flashes outside the airport. For a fraction of a second, everything from the radio tower to the waiting airplanes on the runway is illuminated so brightly against the jet-black sky that it's like looking at a black-and-white portrait. Thunder follows, crackling so loud the ground rattles beneath us. The lights above us flicker. Ruqi grips her brother's hand tight.

"Uh . . ." Feek says slowly. "That . . . didn't sound so good."

The loudspeakers come to staticky life across the terminal. "*Attention all passengers,*" the voice says robotically. "*Due to inclement weather, all flights are grounded until further notice. We repeat, all flights are grounded until further notice.*"

No. No. No.

Breathe in. Breathe out.

It's possible I hallucinated. My anxiety ramped up so high that I imagined my worst-case, deepest-fear scenario. I have to go to the karate competition. I can't miss my flight! But when I look at everyone's pale expressions, I swallow. It's not my imagination.

This is all too horrifyingly real.

And Feek's right. This is not good at all.

AFTER THE ANNOUNCEMENT, THE WHOLE AIRPORT SEEMS TO groan, and Sami takes off with a speed I didn't know the kid had. *How does dude move like a track star in mom jeans?* When Hanna, unbothered, follows me and Ruqi and starts talking about registering for some animal group, I almost grab Ruqi and run too.

Almost, but I remember how Nora talked to Hanna like she was dumb. Like she was a nobody. Like she hadn't dropped everything to find my sister. And I remember how Hanna looked like a puppy who had just been kicked. Seeing that made me think about how Dad left this morning and didn't keep his promise.

I'd barely eaten my fancy dinner last night and I'd gotten in trouble, all so I could perfect lines he said he'd look at after Fajr prayer. But when we finished praying in our hotel room this morning and I pulled out my notebook, Dad pushed it away. Kicking me would have been kinder.

"I have to get to my show," he'd said. Yeah, I knew that. In LA or some other city. What I didn't know—and what I still don't know—is when Dad will return to our home in Philly. This morning was supposed to be my chance. I can't keep track of all his shows. I should have taken a picture of the calendar of Dad's gigs that Mom keeps on the fridge before we left for MONA.

I hold Ruqi's hand tight. Even with all that's happening, she's dancing as I drag her and my own feet to our gate. I kind of miss being little and not caring about anything. Hanna seems upbeat too, and it's . . . strange.

"You going to your gate? To talk to your parents?" I ask.

"My parent. My dad," she corrects me. "No, Dad's fine without me."

"I don't have to check in with my mom either, since I'm about to be a teenager," I say. "I only do it to be nice."

"Let your mom know we're searching for Snickerdoodle. You promised."

"Snickerdoodle! Snickerdoodle! We're finding Cookie Cat!" Ruqi sings.

I quietly pray that Mom doesn't embarrass me and say I can't help Hanna.

Mom is standing and patting Hamza's back when we get to her. "At least he's finally going to sleep," she whispers with a smile. "I got these from the airport as soon as I heard." She motions to two blue foldable cots on the floor.

Nice. Even though we're stuck here, she's in a good mood. Ruqi nuzzles into Mom's side.

I begin working my charm too. "Alhamdulillah, Mom, you can finally put your feet up. Can I get you something?" I motion to Hanna, who's hanging back a little. "I was just going with my friend, Han—"

"Hanna Chen." Hanna walks up, putting out her hand to shake my mom's. "Feek is helping me find Snickerdoodle Mildred Hoffman, a lost cat in the airport."

Mom scrunches up her eyebrows, and I instantly know it's not happening.

"You lost your cat, sweetie? You shouldn't be looking through this big airport by yourself. It's getting late. Where are your parents?"

"My dad is fine. It's not my cat, but Feek, Ruqi, and I are—"

"You, Ruqi, and Feek what?" Mom turns to me accusingly. "Feek, are you playing with strays?"

My ears are burning. "Mom! It's not like that. Snickerdoodle has a family. They're . . . heartbroken!"

"And you're chasing strange cats with your sister and this child too?"

"Hanna's a pro. She finds . . . um . . ." I falter. I can't tell Mom she finds lost sisters.

"Lost loved ones," Hanna says. "I find lost loved ones."

Mom looks back and forth at us with a deep V in her eyebrows.

She finally lands a gentler gaze on Hanna and says, "Sweetie, what you're trying to do is . . . nice, but leave that snicker cat to the experts. Go to your dad. I'm sure he's worried."

"But—" Hanna says.

"Feek and Ruqi are going to sleep now. Good night, child." Mom turns her back. Once again, Hanna looks like she's just been kicked.

I mouth "sorry" to her as her shoulders droop. Then I turn my back like Mom did. I'm not trying to be mean, but I don't want her to see the stupid look on my face. Did Mom have to talk to me like a little kid? In front of go-anywhere-and-do-whatever-she-wants Hanna?

When Hanna is a good number of steps away, I turn and see she's still marching, determined. What's it like to go out and search an airport at night?

Mom carefully places a knocked-out Hamza in his car seat, then sticks out her hand and eyes me meaningfully.

"Here too?" I ask. "We're in an airport. What if I need it?"

"At bedtime, your phone goes away." She repeats the rule I've heard a thousand times.

I groan but take it out. I missed a text from Dad.

Salaams Feekness. Sorry I didn't have time to hear your poem. Send it my way when you get a sec.

Mom clears her throat and snaps. I struggle to hand her my phone without too much attitude. I'm hot right now.

"I hope I can get sleep in this," she mutters as she lies down on one of the cots. She pulls Ruqi beside her and covers them both in a large coat she brought even though it's early September. I try my cot. No way anyone is getting any sleep on one of these.

But within minutes, I hear Mom breathing, deeply asleep. Well, maybe one person can get sleep on these cots.

For me, though, it's time to get back to my rhyme book. I re-read the poem I was going to show Dad this morning, but what I thought sounded good last night feels messy and weak to me now. Maybe it was a blessing I didn't get to share it?

No, I *am* good at this. I flip to the lines I wrote before Ruqi disappeared earlier: *I'm the words to the song/ The hammer to the gong/ The beats to this rhythm* . . .

What rhymes with "rhythm"? Think! But I still got nothing. It's like Ruqi has blocked me. How does Dad rhyme even when he's constantly going and constantly tired? I write what I wish I could ask him:

Dear Dad,
Do lines drop down incomplete for you too?
Do your rhymes forget the beat, 'cause mine do?
Do you read your stuff and pray for better?
~~Do you go back to cross out every letter?~~
~~Do you go back and erase every letter?~~

Ugh! My poem about not flowing doesn't flow. I draw a big X over the lines. The answer is "no" to my questions, anyway. Dad can do poetry half asleep. I'll have to figure out how to do that too.

"Shiny house!" Ruqi peeks her head out from Mom's coat and points to that big ridiculous machine.

"Ruqi," I groan. "Now is not the time."

"Cookie Cat!"

"You still thinking about Snickerdoodle?"

"Snickerdoodle! Snickerdoodle!" she sings.

"Shhh!" I look at Mom and Hamza, still soundly asleep. "You heard Mom—we can't look for Snickerdoodle. Want to see some cat videos?"

Thankfully, she comes to my cot.

I sigh when I reach into my empty pocket. I forgot I don't have my phone.

"Shiny house!" Ruqi jumps up.

I pull her back down. "Ruqi, I know it's cool that the balls are moving and all, but we have to stay here." How does Mom usually make her sleepy? "Lay down. I'll . . . tell you a bedtime story."

Ruqi looks skeptical. "We don't have no books here."

"It's in here." I point to my head.

She squints at me. "What's it about?"

"A superhero named Feek."

"No," she says.

"Fine, a unicorn."

She claps. "And Snickerdoodle. And my fwiend Nora!"

"Okay, sure. Once there were three friends, Ruqayyah the unicorn, Snickerdoodle the cat, and Nora the evil, foul-smelling witch—"

"Nora, the pwetty pwincess," Ruqi corrects.

"Fine! Once there were three friends: Ruqayyah the unicorn, Snickerdoodle the Cat, and Nora the *okay*-looking princess with probably no foul smells," I begin again and finally, thank God almighty, she lies down to listen.

But do you know I'm only five minutes into my story—a rousing, powerful bedtime story—and Ruqi starts looking around? From her pocket, she digs out that paper she ripped from Hanna's flier and looks at that instead. My story is more boring than a flier?

I snatch the paper. "I thought you wanted a story."

"Cookie Cat!" Ruqi reaches for the paper.

Groan. This again. I'm about to just give her the stupid flier when something catches my eye. I see the cat—or half of it, since the paper's ripped—with its back paws on a floor with golden geometric designs. I've only seen a floor like that at Doc Hoffa's house. Is that floor common? It looked unique to me.

"Gimme Cookie Cat back!"

Cookie Cat. Suddenly, I'm back at Doc Hoffa's house. At a party with almost a hundred guests from the poetry industry and their families, celebrating the premiere of *Storm the Stage*.

Mom had whisper-shouted at Ruqi, "Leave that cat alone. That's Cookie's cat."

Cookie.

I thought it was funny that Lala Hoffa, wife of Doc Hoffa and former supermodel, was going by that name. Doc Hoffa kept calling her "Cookie" and she kept calling him "Hoffa Choc-a Chip." She almost purred it. Yeah, ridiculous. It gets better. When she would call her kids—and I couldn't keep track of them all in that crowd—she would call them some silly cookie name.

She'd say, "Shortbread, hunny, don't pick your nose" or "Biscotti, baby, tie your shoes" or "Where's Fortune? Anyone seen

Fortune?" or "Come give Mommy a kissy kiss, Gingersnap." I think I even heard a "Mealy Raisin."

But did I hear a Snickerdoodle? I don't know. I was taking it all in: the guests, the golden floor, the gigantic crystal chandelier, famous poets casually strolling through rooms, and a six-foot-tall supermodel running after kids but never toppling in six-inch heels. At least one floofy-looking cat was walking around, but who except Ruqi cares about a cat in Doc Hoffa's mansion? Could Snickerdoodle be their cat?

I look back at the flier again. CONTACT COOKIE HOFFMAN, it says. I think I've read somewhere that Doc Hoffa's real last name is Hoffman. Cookie probably doesn't want to use her celebrity name. I get that. Even though my dad is a small celebrity, it's sometimes more convenient not to tell people who he is. Dad told us before attending their party that he signed an agreement that we wouldn't take pictures or share details, because people always make up horrible stories about the Hoffas for gossip sites. I'm thinking about the online search I'll do when I get my phone back in the morning when I look up to see Ruqi already a few steps away.

I jump up and grab her.

"Not so fast!" And then I almost beg, "Listen to the rest of the story, Ruqi."

"Okay," Ruqi says, before lying back down on my cot. But I don't trust her "okay."

Please let her go to sleep!

IF DAD—SITTING ACROSS FROM ME AT OUR GATE, WHERE I'VE been banished to by Feek's mom—wasn't shooting me guilty glances in between reading something on his iPad, I'd ask him a deep question. Usually he's good with such questions, the type that take a lot of talking to get to the right answer.

But now the look on his face tells me he's thinking about his secret matrimonial quest from the weekend.

If he was his normal self, I'd ask him, *Do the ends ever justify the means if the ends end up saving a life?*

Like if you're about to do an illegal thing but it's for something good, isn't that okay?

Like, can I pretend to be thirteen and make a Facebook account in order to check in with the Hoffmans?

I desperately need to connect with them. And I can't use Dad's account anymore because he changed his password, and I couldn't crack it even after trying all his other passwords.

When I checked the Animal Allies forum on my phone, I learned that the Hoffmans had updated their Facebook page *just an hour ago* about two new potential sightings of Snickerdoodle at Hurston today.

More.

Snickerdoodle.

Sightings. *Today.*

Now I'm convinced that flights getting canceled is heaven-sent. Isn't Allah giving me another message? *Here are some extra hours to find Snickerdoodle?*

I don't want to waste a second of it.

So during all this time sitting here, I've tried my hardest to reach RainingCatsNDogs, the person who posted about the new Snickerdoodle sightings on the Animal Allies forum, but so far, they haven't replied to any of my messages. They didn't post any information on the locations where Snickerdoodle may have been last seen! (I'm pretty sure they assumed everyone could just go check the Facebook links themselves. Not remembering that some Animal Allies members are under the age of thirteen. Sob.)

Which means I need to go right to the source! I desperately need to talk to the Hoffmans *themselves* so they can tell me where I should focus my investigations.

I bring up the MAKE AN ACCOUNT Facebook window on my phone browser that I'd already filled in with my name and other extremely truthful details, except for the entry for year in the date-of-birth field. (It says I was born two years earlier than I was. Because sometimes you gotta do what you gotta do.)

Before clicking submit, I look up at Dad to see if he's watching.

Oh great. We end up exchanging guilty glances.

I close the browser window.

He puts down his iPad. "Was the food court busy? What did you get to eat?"

I go back to the Animal Allies forum on my phone to see if RainingCatsNDogs has responded to my twelve messages and posts.

"Nothing," I murmur to myself.

"A whole food court and you didn't find anything?" Dad says, putting his iPad away in his laptop bag. He stands up and puts the bag on his shoulder. "Want to come with me now and get something? Before the restaurants close?"

"No, I'm okay."

Instead of making his way to the food court, he comes over and crouches in front of me. "Hanna, *are* you okay?"

Uh-oh. He says that with so much sadness that my throat gets plugged and hot tears attack the back of my eyes and I want to yell, "NO! I'M NOT OKAY. I'M IN AGONY. IN ANGUISH. YOU WENT TO FIND A NEW MOM FOR ME AT THE CONFERENCE WITHOUT TELLING ME. SO HOW IN THIS UNJUST WORLD CAN I BE OKAY?!?"

But I hold it in and don't answer. He will get nothing from me. And then nothing will happen.

Like Dad getting married.

To make the lump in my throat disappear, I stare at the logo for Animal Allies—a dog, cat, and bird flying a plane together, waving—and try to think about that precious future moment when I finally find Snickerdoodle (insha'Allah) and give her a handful of Meow Mix treats from *my* hands.

"I want to talk to you about something, actually," Dad says, taking his laptop bag off his shoulder and setting it down on the floor by his legs.

He's getting comfy.

I look up. I need to escape.

"I was going to wait until we got to Auntie Lisa's, but we have time now." He's lifting an arm like he's getting ready to . . . hug me?

Comfort me?

When he tells me the awful truth—that I'm getting a new mom?

Even though I've never gotten a chance to know my real mom and I'm still learning about her. Even though I still love her so much.

It feels like alarm bells and huge sirens are going off in my brain: GO! LEAVE! WHILE YOU STILL CAN!

RUN!!!

I get up.

"What are you doing? What's wrong, Hanna?" He's reaching out. His hand brushes my elbow. "The whole weekend you've been ignoring me. I thought it was because you were busy with your friends, but now what's happening?"

Sami.

I can make out his sky-blue shirt out of the corner of my eye. He's at a set of seats at the gate across.

It's like it's waving at me, his shirt. Even though his face is actually super-frowny above his shirt as he stares hard at the tablet he's clutching, it's still a nice, friendly sign.

He never got a chance to answer if he's on board to help me find Snickerdoodle. Feek said he was in, but then his mom didn't understand the mission.

Sigh. Feek would have been super helpful—the way he just knows what he's talking about. And the way he trusts me.

Sami, I'm not so sure about. His forehead scrunches a lot like he's calculating a ton of things in his head.

But I guess Sami will have to do. Beggars can't be choosers.

"I wish you'd talk to me." Dad rests a hand on my shoulder gently.

Oh noooo. A big part of me wants to sink into that hand and let Dad hug me tight, like when I used to cry about not knowing who to make Mother's Day cards for at school.

Back then, I was really crying because everyone in my class knew two things: one, that I didn't have a mother to make a card for, and two, all the teachers brought up "you can even make a card for your grandma or an aunt or a neighbor" just because I, Hanna Chen, was in the class.

Dad said it was okay if I made Mother's Day into a little joke for myself. That I could make up imaginary people to make funny cards for, like "thank you for knitting me socks from dryer lint" or "you make the bitterest radish cake in the entire world" or "you're the best great-great-great-great-grandma!"

Then we'd make a real card for Mom at home, with my big brother, Adam, helping sometimes too. It was full of prayers for her in heaven and current pictures of me because she'd never seen me older than a baby.

And Dad makes sure to hug me tight all the days leading up to every Mother's Day, and all the days after, until I put away Mom's card from that year with the other cards in a box.

I know I'll never be able to give them to her, but I also know I don't ever want to make cards for any other mother either.

Even if Dad found someone else.

I stand and move away from his hand.

Sami! He just looked up at me!

"Wait, where are you going?" Now Dad stands, his voice bewildered.

"One of my friends is waving me over. He needs help," I say over my shoulder, holding up my phone. "You can text me if you need me, Dad."

I make sure I don't turn around. I don't want him to see my face, and I for sure don't want to see his. I know both of our faces are sad, and seeing Dad's will make the tears filling my eyes just spill.

I can't cry when I have things to do.

I'm so glad Snickerdoodle needs me to find her.

And that Sami will help me.

CHAPTER 11

SAMI

THIS ISN'T HAPPENING.

This can't be happening.

I need to get to the bus stop in NINE hours!

"Sami, take a deep breath," says my mother as the sound of thunder crackles so loudly the windows tremble.

"Seriously, kiddo." My father pats my back and looks at me worriedly. "In and out—like we've talked about."

"But it's storming so *bad* outside!"

He looks out the large glass windows. "It *is* pretty rough out there, but don't worry, we're safe here."

My mother nods. "As scary as it is, the airport is built to withstand a storm like this."

Scary? They think I'm scared the lightning storm is going to personally zap me? I look at them. They think I'm a scaredy-cat too, don't they?

"No, th-that's not what I meant," I manage to say. "D-do you think there's at least a *chance* the plane might take off? I know it won't be on time now, but the storm *could* pass quickly. And if they board us in the next few hours, we'd still have a chance—"

My words are interrupted by a crackle of thunder like a pop-corn machine going berserk, followed by an emphatic *BOOM*. The lights in the airport flicker again.

I guess I have my answer . . . but . . .

"*Other* airports!" I exclaim. "Let's look up an airport out of the storm path? We could take a different flight."

"Sami—" my mother begins.

"There won't be any flights until morning," Dad tells me.

"But if the flight is in the morning, I'll miss the bus. It leaves at six o'clock sharp, and Sensei told us he wasn't going to wait for anyone."

"Yeahhh." My dad makes a sympathetic face. "If I'm going to guess, according to the hourly forecast on my weather app, our flight won't take off until five or six in the morning, when the storm clouds clear."

Five. Or six. In the morning. My brain feels like it's glitching. Because five or six in the morning means we won't get back to Orlando by late morning. Which means I am missing not only the epic bus ride up to Gainesville with my teammates but the karate competition too.

"I know this is disappointing. You've worked so hard." Mom glances at my dad and then back at me. "Might be a good time to just take your mind off things? Why don't you catch up on some Zelda?"

"Let me know if you get stuck with the divine beast," Dad says. "I have a trick for that."

Do they really think playing a video game will help me feel better about missing the most important competition of my life?

Thunder clangs outside, but I don't even flinch. I'm numb. Like someone's dipped me in a bucket of ice water. Even the prospect of unlimited Switch time can't make me feel better.

I pull out my tablet and text Ibrahim.

Well the worst-case scenario came true this time. Our flight is canceled and my karate competition is not happening.

Miraculously, the text goes through. I stare at the text box, waiting for an answer, when out of the corner of my eye, I spot Hanna. She's close by—and I'm pretty sure she's looking intently in my direction.

"Psst! Sami, over here!"

Okay, she's *definitely* looking in my direction.

But I'm not in the mood to talk about Snickerdoodle. (I'm 99.99 percent sure that's what she's here about.) I need to figure out *some* way back to Orlando.

Maybe . . . I feel a glimmer of hope. We could do something like in the movie *Home Alone*. The one with the kid who gets left behind by his family. His mom ended up getting a ride in a rental truck with a band of polka players to reach him. We're not going to hitchhike with a band of musicians, of course, but maybe we could rent a car? That's it! I'll find nearby rental car companies and present them to my parents. There's no way my parents will say no if I hand them the solution on a silver platter.

I type in "rental cars" and grimace. The Wi-Fi is out again.

"Sami?" My mother nudges me. "I think there's someone here for you."

I look up—it's Hanna. Right here. Her arms are folded. And she's smiling.

"Looks like our gates are near each other," she says. "That's pretty cool."

"Uh. Yeah," I say. "Cool."

I've known Hanna for approximately five minutes, but I'm reasonably certain she's not here to make small talk.

"Soooo." Hanna tilts her head. "I was thinking . . . since we're stranded here anyway, would you be up for helping me?"

And *there* it is. But luckily, while she was talking, I was coming up with my own counterpoints of why I could *not* help. A) I am trying to figure out some important stuff of my own (which is true); B) it is late (also true); and C) my parents don't want me out and about just because the flight isn't going on as scheduled.

And that is the moment when my mother absolutely and completely betrays me by saying, "Sami would *love* to help you."

I stare at her, sending her the clearest subliminal, telepathic message I possibly can that I have my own important mission to figure out. But both Hanna and my mother are beaming.

"You . . . don't even know what she wants me to help with."

"There's a missing cat in the airport," Hanna explains to my mother. "Snickerdoodle. I have some ideas where she might be, and I could definitely use an extra set of eyes."

Instead of frowning and asking Hanna why she is taking it upon herself to do this, my mother nods like this is the most logical thing in the world and says, "Sure, Sami loves animals. He has two rabbits, Lucy and Ethel." Completely ignoring my death-ray eyes lasering in on her, she turns to me and says, "We'll be here Sami-bug—and yes, I know." She raises a palm, completely misunderstanding my stare. "If by some miracle they let flights take off before morning, there'll be an announcement. Go on and spend some time with your friend. It'll make the waiting go faster."

My friend. My chest tightens. So that's what this is about. Of course it is. They think I've made a buddy. Why am I surprised? She always does this.

Hanna's looking earnestly at me. My mother's still smiling. I stuff my tablet in my book bag, sling it over my shoulder, and get up. I'll go for a little bit, then head back to figure out the rental car situation.

"Where are we going?" I ask as we walk away. "Did you get some kind of lead or something?"

"Not really." Her eyes wander over to the other gates around us. "But I figure we can start by interviewing employees . . . and . . ."

I see where she's looking. Feek's at the gate near the Rube Goldberg marble machine thingy. His mom is asleep. I see a little baby asleep too. But Feek's wide-awake, sitting on a cot, looking resignedly at his little sister next to him, who is also super awake.

She's eyeing them wistfully. Was I plan B after Feek? Or plan C after Feek *and* Ruqi?

"I don't get why he can't help." Hanna shakes her head. "It's not like we're going to wander into traffic—it's an airport!"

There it is. I swallow. She tried him first and he said no. I *am* the backup plan, and even though I'm not surprised, the confirmation hurts.

"She might not even be here anymore," I tell her. "She could've slipped out of the airport. Got on a plane or something?"

Hanna shakes her head firmly. "Someone thinks they spotted her just a little while ago! She's here. She's definitely here."

I'm slowly realizing resistance is futile. Hanna is on a mission, and I am apparently now part of that mission, even if I am option C.

I see Ruqi perk up in the distance. She's looking at something past our shoulders. Glancing back, I realize it's not a something, but a some*one*. Nora. She's got her headphones on, and she's completely absorbed with something on her phone. (Is her Wi-Fi working?! Maybe she'd be up for letting me use it for just a minute . . . ?)

"Nora!" Ruqi squeals from across the hall. She turns to her brother. "That's my fwiend!"

"Your friend?" I hear Feek snort.

"*Our* fwiend. She bought me a Cinna-Yum!"

Hanna moves toward them. "I think I'm going to ask him again. If at first you don't succeed, try, try again."

Before she can reach Feek, Ruqi's up and running toward Nora's gate. Feek jumps up and chases Ruqi. Hanna hurries after Feek. My tablet buzzes in my book bag. Ibrahim just replied.

Aw bummer, but no big deal, there'll be other competitions. No need to get all squirrelly. It's not the end of the world.

The words land like a gut punch. Squirrelly. Sami the squirrel. He hasn't called me that in years. But it lands just like it did when I was five. When I stared too long at the Dumbo ride at Disney World and lost my family for the longest twenty-two seconds of my life. I'd been crying uncontrollably when my parents and brother finally retraced their steps back to me. Those were the words he'd spoken. He'd only ever used them a few times. And he's using them now.

Shake it off, I tell myself. I walk toward the others. It's one thing for kids at school to call me Sami the Scaredy-Cat, but it hurts to know that's how my family sees me too. Someone who's afraid a thunderstorm's going to zap him while he's sitting inside an airport. Someone who freaks out. Someone who can't get a grip. And considering I was her last choice, it's pretty obvious Hanna thinks so too.

That's why this karate competition was so important. It was a chance to prove that I'm *not* squirrelly. I'm not a scaredy-cat. I can do a roundhouse kick better than anyone in my age group. I'm the youngest purple belt the dojo's ever had. And tomorrow my brother and my parents were going to see just how good I can be at something.

But that's not happening now.

And maybe it's for the best.

You can't just put on a karate uniform and change who you are. At the end of the day, the closest I'll ever get to being brave is in a video game. In real life, no matter what I might try to do, I'm still me. I'm still Sami.

THERE'S NO WAY I'M GETTING HOME IN TIME FOR MY PARTY.

The rain is coming down hard and loud. People are sitting everywhere, spread out on the floor, leaning against the walls and their luggage.

I have a seat because Mom saved one for me. She's answering emails, and I'm scrolling through NokNok when I get a message from Sumaya that makes my stomach drop.

Real nice, Nora/Noora, you told me you weren't having a birthday party.

Below the message is a forwarded post—with a countdown to my party. Mackenzie and Kennedy post about everything. I should've known I'd get caught in a lie.

I groan, and Mom thinks it's about missing my party.

"Don't worry about the delay. We'll reschedule as soon as we can."

"I don't care about rescheduling," I say. "Just cancel it." I keep my tone flat, but I'm frustrated. There's so much more going on here than a stupid birthday party. I might have told her about it if we'd had more than ten minutes alone together this entire weekend.

"Why, habibti, what's wrong? It's your thirteenth birthday. That's a special one. Did something happen between you and the girls?"

I stare at my phone's home screen. It bugs me that she's calling me "my love" in Arabic. It's my grandmother's pet name for me, but even thinking of my sittee is not enough to override the urge to say something sarcastic like, "Why do I even need a party when I just had such a special birthday weekend at the Chocolate Garden?"

But before I can say anything, Ruqi comes charging through the crowd of people at our gate.

"Ruqi! Are you lost again?" I call out before I see Hanna, Feek, and Sami trailing behind her.

Mom looks surprised that I remembered Ruqi's name from the conference, but I offer nothing by way of explanation. I don't want to give her the satisfaction of thinking that I made friends on this trip. Mom says, "It's my future intern."

"She's not lost!" Feek says and grabs Ruqi's hand.

Sami is quiet, standing behind Hanna while she introduces herself and gushes over how much she admires Mom. "I also want to be a force of change in the world," she adds, "and right now my mission in life is to save animals lost in airports."

Hanna explains about Snickerdoodle, and even though I can tell that Mom is caught off guard by Hanna's passionate, impromptu speech, she doesn't show it. Congressmom always looks interested in the requests she gets.

But when Hanna concludes her mini-presentation with, "So, Nora, can you help us look for Snickerdoodle?" Mom surprises me. She doesn't put Hanna or her cause first. Instead, she says, "Wow, this sounds like such a worthwhile issue, and I love your enthusiasm, Hanna. But perhaps Nora can join you later. We were in the middle of discussing something important."

It's unlike Mom to put our time together before others, and it makes me so uncomfortable that my skin itches. Where was all this concern when I was alone and without any friends at the conference or when we were trying to make it to the Chocolate Garden? She just wants to ask me more questions about what's going on with my friends at school, and the last thing I want to do is tell her.

The truth is I did something really unkind to Sumaya. One day, I was in the bathroom with Mackenzie and Kennedy, and we were freshening up our hair. First, Mackenzie said something like, "Can you imagine being like that girl Sumaya and not being able to style your hair?" Then Kennedy added that she thought it would be so boring to have to wear this thing on your head every day and not change your look, and I joined in and said, "Yeah, and imagine trying to shop. Her clothing options must be so limited."

Then out came Sumaya from the stall right behind us. She heard the whole thing, and instead of apologizing, I let Sumaya defend herself and say, "And I can't imagine spending my lunch break in the bathroom talking about people. Especially my own people." She made air quotes with her fingers and added, "Noora Najjar," with an Arabic accent, just the way my grandma and sometimes my mom say my name.

After she washed her hands and left, Mackenzie asked me why Sumaya said my name like that, and I shrugged. Later I regretted it. That was the moment when I should have told Mackenzie and Kennedy about my family's background.

That night, I messaged Sumaya on NokNok, but it got ugly real fast. She said I was an Arab who'd forgotten where I came from and that I probably didn't even know that my name is supposed to be pronounced Noora, not Nora, and that it means "light" in Arabic.

I told Sumaya the truth—that my grandparents were born in Michigan and there were a lot of things I didn't know about my ancestry because there was a lot my parents didn't know either.

Sumaya was surprised. She said that her family came to the US from Iraq when she was seven and that she didn't know there were Muslims and Arabs who had been here for generations.

Somehow after sharing all that, we got to messaging about other stuff—school, family, baking. Turns out Sumaya's a sweetie too, and we started sending each other recipes and pictures of desserts we'd made. But at school, I didn't tell anyone we'd become friends. As my birthday drew closer, she asked me directly if I was having a party. I lied and said no because I thought it would have been worse for her to know that she wasn't invited.

But now I see that finding out from someone else was definitely worse.

"Come on, Hanna," Feek whispers. "We don't need her to find Snickerdoodle." He turns to leave.

I'm about to lose my chance to get away.

"That's okay, Mom," I say. "We can talk later."

I put out my hand and let Ruqi pull me to her side. I don't know where we're going or what cat-obsessed thing these kids are up to next, but doing just about anything in this airport sounds better than waiting here.

Zora Neale Hurston Airport

Case Notes - Hanna A. Chen

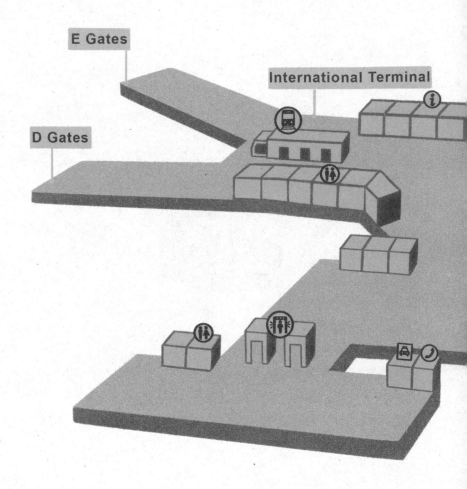

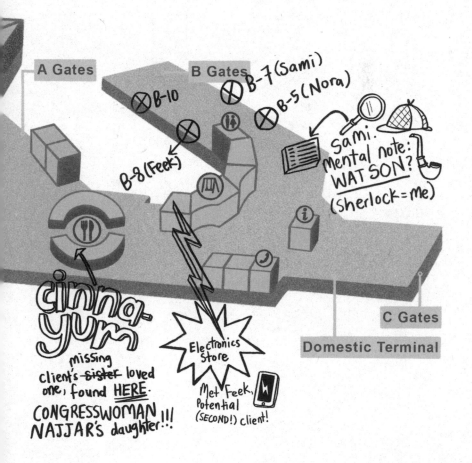

I FEEL LIKE I'M IN THAT PAINTING *LIBERTY LEADING THE PEOPLE* that my art teacher showed the class last year. (I'm Liberty, of course. Holding up a flag—with the logo of Animal Allies—for all to follow.)

I turn to check if they're still following me, and what I see fills me with pride. Puffy pride.

Sami and Feek (Feek! Clutching the ripped LOST SNICKERDOODLE flier!) are marching behind me, and they both have the same look on their faces: EXCITEMENT.

They are as excited about finding Snickerdoodle as I am.

I glance back again. Yup, even Nora, who's being pulled along by Ruqi, has a determined look in her eyes.

"There it is!" I yell. "The Zoomi store!" I half run, half speed-walk to the luggage store across the food court.

Just as we were leaving Congresswoman Sarah Najjar, RainingCatsNDogs finally responded to my messages and told me that Snickerdoodle may have last been seen at the Zoomi store! (A message I almost missed because I had my phone on vibrate only! You bet that after this, I turned the volume ALL THE WAY UP!)

It felt so good to tell everyone that I had an actual solid, real, true lead.

When we get to the luggage store, I pause to address them all. "Okay, this might be a historic moment. Several airports have lost several—actually hundreds, or, maybe, if we count all the airports all around the world, thousands of animals. Only a fraction of those animals are ever found." I pause for dramatic effect.

Nora, who's come to a stop behind Sami and Feek, convinces me to keep my speech short and sweet by the way her eyes move from determined to skeptical—again.

I don't have much time. "This may be a historic moment because we get to help increase that fraction of found pets. *We*," I say. "We the—"

"Please don't say *we the people*," Nora interrupts.

"I wasn't going to. I was going to say we the . . . the ones who care . . . we can join together to help find a poor lost cat in"—I point to Zoomi—"that store. Where she was last seen. That's why this is a historic moment. Very few lost airport animals get found by travelers. Travelers who care. Like you."

"Wow, you sound like my mom," Nora says with a slight smile on her face. "Are you sure you're not running for office?"

Maybe she's making fun of me, maybe that's actually a smirk on her face and not a slight smile, but I'm thrilled Nora connected what I said to *her* mom, a person who's actually changing the world every single day. (Though, when I met her mom a little while ago, she turned down a new opportunity to change the world. But I just *know* if I had had a few more minutes with

Congresswoman Sarah Najjar, she would have been onboard with my plans to ensure the safety of flying pets.)

I pivot to face the store, the others now flanking me. "Okay, let's go. If you see anything suspicious, record it. Even the slightest thing. We're looking for evidence of a cat hiding in the store in the recent past. So look everywhere. And, again, record!"

"I don't have my phone on me, so you guys will have to record," Feek says. "But I'll look around carefully."

Sami puts up his hand, the one that's not holding his iPad. "But are we even allowed? To record inside a store like that?"

"And how likely is it that the cat would still be there?" Nora asks, her eyes boring into mine.

"Snickerdoodle may have been at Zoomi's an hour ago. She could still be there. But if she's not, recording video is important. We could look at the footage later and see if we missed anything. And Sami, we're allowed to take pictures inside stores. I'm pretty sure." I march toward Zoomi, still giving directions, but at a murmur now. "Let's keep it quiet—don't bring attention to yourselves. In case they figure out we're not just customers. And in case they treat us like kids. But I'll be talking to the person who works here to get some more background."

"But wouldn't *that* look suspicious?" It's Sami again. I knew he was the type of kid in class who said "BUT THIS" and "BUT THAT" a lot during group work.

"Don't worry, I'll be professional about it. Let's do this," I whisper as we step into the store.

Ruqi stops suddenly and yells, "I need to use the bathwoom!"

"Right now?" Feek shakes his head. "Can't you hold it for just five minutes while we look around?"

"I need to go nowwww!"

"You guys go on ahead," Nora says. "I'll take her. I'm pretty sure *none of us* wants her to go by herself and get lost again."

Nora looks at Feek pointedly when she says the "none of us" part.

"Oh—okay, thanks?" Feek says, pausing to watch Ruqi yank Nora away. He shakes his head, and I give him an "it's okay, let it go" pat on his arm.

Feek gives me a nod and heads to the back of the store. Which is smart because Sami is lingering around the front, looking at a sporty duffel bag wistfully for some reason. He looks like a bunny that needs a hug, and I feel weirdly sad for a moment, like I should go over and check if he's okay.

But then I see the employee standing behind the counter. He's staring off into the distance, not really noticing us. Maybe that's because his floppy brown hair almost covers his eyes. He looks like he's way older than my brother, Adam, like maybe in his twenties or even older. He's got on a white shirt with a skinny black tie and skinny pants.

I need to get to work. I carefully make my way around the perimeter of the store, my eyes scanning from top to bottom like I'm vacuuming in neat rows.

Once I finish zigzagging the middle of the store with my phone, I glance at the employee again. He's still staring ahead.

I make my way to the counter. "Hi."

He nods, his hands in his pockets as he leans against the shelf of purses behind him.

"So," I start, "we're looking for something."

He still doesn't glance at me. Does he have earbuds in his ears under his floppy hair? Is he listening to music or a podcast? Sometimes Adam does that while I'm trying to talk to him.

"But it's not luggage, *actually*. That we're looking for." I emphasize "actually" to draw his attention to me. "It's *actually* a cat."

He finally looks down at me. "Are you kids here with an adult?"

"No . . ." I lean across the counter to read his name tag. "Jake. We're not here with an adult. But you can still help us, right?"

"Look for your cat?" He shakes his head. "No, that's not my job."

"No, not *my* cat. But Snickerdoodle, you might know about her? The missing airport cat?" I give a quick glance around the store to check on Sami and Feek.

I give a discreet thumbs-up to Sami, who's now looking at a rack of messenger bags.

I can't see Feek from where I'm standing, but I hear the odd noise here and there that lets me know he's rolling some cases. We're the only people in the shop, so it's kind of like being in a museum, where every sound is really sharp.

"Oh, I see. You saw the news about the latest lost pet and are trying to play detective." Jake pulls his hands out of the skinny pockets with some difficulty and crosses his arms.

"She was last seen here," I point out. "Did you notice anything?"

"An idea: Why don't we let the airport take care of finding the cat?" Jake raises his eyebrows. Like he's making a really good point, the same point Sami has made many times before.

But it's not a good point because the airport has been looking for a week and they haven't found anything.

"Over here, Hanna!" Feek yells from the back corner. "I found something."

I rush over, with Jake following behind, suddenly activated.

Feek is pointing at a hard navy-blue carry-on. There's a dusty-looking patch at the top, near the handle.

I bend over to take a closer look, running my finger on the patch a few times. That's not dust like I first thought; it's a lighter blue layer exposed underneath the outer case of the luggage.

Like what happens when sharp, catty claws scratch something hard.

"So Snickerdoodle *is* here!" I turn to Jake, unable to stop the accusatory tone in my voice, my fingers stabbing the suitcase. "This is a cat scratch."

Jake bends over and examines the scratch too. And then he looks straight at Feek. "What did you do?"

"Me?" Feek's face floods with emotion—shock, fear, and then anger. "I didn't do this!"

"Before you got here, this was a perfectly good suitcase." Jake shakes his head, his eyes piercing Feek's like he's pinning him in place. "And now it's destroyed."

Destroyed? I can't believe what's happening. Jake is *actually* accusing Feek of scratching the luggage! I frown and shake my head hard. "No, Mr. Jake. Feek didn't do this."

"Well, it's not a cat that did it." Jake points at the scratch. "This has been made with something broad, like a ring or something, not pointy cat nails. Which would be in stripes."

Jake shoots a glance at the silver crescent ring on Feek's thumb.

Feek curls up his hand, his fingers enclosing his ring in response.

"If this was a perfectly good suitcase, why is it in the clearance section?" Feek asks, pointing at the red LAST CHANCE SALE sign attached to the shelf, under which more navy-blue suitcases sit. I nod my head triumphantly.

Jake doesn't answer. Instead he yanks his head toward the front entrance to the store, his arms back to being crossed at his chest. "Did you guys maybe notice, when you snuck in, that the gate was partly down? Which was a message for you to NOT come inside unless you're actually going to be spending money? Because we're closing in ten minutes? So exit now! Instead of scratching the luggage and blaming it on a lost cat!"

I can't stop myself from glaring at him. "We have a right to look around the store," I say, louder this time so Sami hears too. "So no thanks, we're not leaving. We'll keep looking around."

"Hanna, let's just go." Feek pulls both his hands into fists and shoves them into his hoodie pockets. His face is a mixture of hurt and anger.

"But we can shop here too," I appeal to Feek, my hands on my hips. *Feek and me and Sami have a right to be treated just like any other customer.*

"And what type of luggage are you 'shopping' for exactly?" Jakc makes air quotes when he says "shopping."

I look around. Sami is examining the duffel bags again. I raise my voice even louder. "A sports bag, right, Sami? We're looking for a sports bag?"

Sami shakes his head, and I raise my eyebrows and nod quickly to let him know that's the wrong answer. He nods and says, "Yes, a bag for my karate tournament."

"Really? And you want a *five-hundred-dollar luxury*-brand gym bag for karate?" Jake raises his eyebrows. "Okay, I've had enough. I need to start closing up the shop. Out you go!"

Why is he exploding? Jake must know something.

His skinny tie and skinny pants and skinny pockets know something about Snickerdoodle.

For him to go from being an expressionless robot to screaming at us in literally ten minutes . . .

Feek shakes his head and mutters something under his breath and starts making his way to the entrance, but I put a hand out to stop him. "There's four more minutes until store closing, so let's keep investigating." I look ahead to find . . . Sami? Where's Sami?

He's standing right outside the store, staring back at us. He probably took off when Jake started blowing up.

"Listen, did anyone tell you that you need to learn manners?" Jake makes shooing motions like me and Feek are a couple of flies—*while he's talking to us about manners.* "*You* especially." He points at me. "Didn't your mom ever teach you to respect adults? Or did she forget about that part?"

I stare at Jake for a moment and then turn away quickly as I feel my eyes getting hot.

Oh no, my lips are trembling.

Why did Jake have to bring up Mom?

It's going to take me off my mission.

I can feel all the puffy pride deflating.

I feel limp.

Feek looks at me, and this time he pats my arm. "I said, let's go, Hanna." He tips his head to the front of the store.

"Ah, someone who actually listens," Jake says. "Maybe you can give your friend here some pointers!"

When we get to the front of the store, me wiping my eyes before Sami sees them too, Feek turns around to Jake. "Pointers? I'll give you some pointers. You are the worst store employee I've ever met. Your manners are uglier than them pants. Your breath stinks and you—"

"Get out or I'm calling security!" The man moves like he's going to lunge toward us, and we leap out the door.

The metal grate clangs shut behind us so hard, we run.

CHAPTER 14

FEEK

WE RUN ONLY A FEW FEET BEFORE HANNA SLOWS, STOPS, then sits (almost drops, if I'm being honest) on the floor. I don't know what else to do, so I sit across from her. Is she about to cry? Sami looks back at Zoomi and then back at us, eyes wide. Before he can speak, I shake my head. He closes his eyes, takes a breath, then sits too. We stare, but none of us see each other.

Instead, I see the way that man looked at me. Like I was a criminal. He's probably racist, hates Muslims for sure. Black Muslims even more.

He'll give us some pointers? We're doing real things, trying to save animals and help heartbroken families. He's just selling ugly bags and sporting cheap skinny jeans and bad hair to look half his age, but somehow he's better than us?

"It's just me on my own. And I don't know how to do anything right," Hanna says, like she's muttering to herself.

"Hanna, you're not on your own. We're with you . . . Why are you upset?" I ask, confused.

"I . . . I forgot what a cat scratch looks like." And, yeah, she's crying. I don't really get it, but then again, I know what it is to care a lot about something others don't get.

Sami and I exchange glances, both of us silently asking the other to say something to make this whole thing better. But I got nothing. Sami opens his mouth but then closes it and looks away. I guess he's got nothing too.

I clear my throat. "It was one mistake."

"I couldn't tell a cat scratch from a human one. That's huge."

"Are you sure Jake was telling the truth? I mean, first he tried to blame it on us. And then, when he couldn't prove it, he looked nervous, like he was hiding something."

"I saw that too," Sami says.

"He wants us to feel like a bunch of dumb kids," I say, getting mad again. "What if it's because we're right?"

"But how can I be sure we're on the trail? I examined every inch of that store. No cat hair. Not a single one." Hanna sniffles.

"We didn't get to see all of the store. What if Snickerdoodle went behind the counter?" I ask, trying to rally her.

At this, Hanna swipes at her tears and stands. "You're right . . . you're right . . . but how do we get in to see?"

Sami shoots up. "Wait, let's think about—"

I jump up too. We can do this. "Maybe I can talk another employee into letting us in."

"But—" Sami says.

"What if we're still wrong?" Hanna's voice wavers. Where did the Hanna I met earlier go?

"What if we're right?" I'm almost pleading. "Come on, Hanna. Don't get knocked down by people like that Jake guy." Something about seeing someone like Hanna so thoroughly defeated messes with me. I make a lot of mistakes. Our mistakes don't mean we should give up, do they?

We can't just quit, especially knowing who Snickerdoodle belongs to. Should I tell them? *But the Hoffmans chose to not share their identities for a reason.*

"Snickerdoodle! Snickerdoodle!" Ruqi sings out. She's holding on to Nora's hand while skipping over to us, and Nora kind of skips with her. Ruqi can't simply walk like a normal person. I roll my eyes, but Nora is giggling. Nora sees me looking and switches to an all-about-business walk.

Hanna gives Ruqi a watery smile.

Ruqi smiles back at Hanna and opens her palm. "Don't cwy. This is for you!"

Hanna gasps.

"That's a—" Sami gapes.

"No way," Nora whispers.

"What? What is this?" I take the silver trinket from her hand.

"A cat collar bell. Gucci, my cat, has one just like it," Nora says.

"You have a cat named Gucci?" Hanna asks excitedly.

I snort at this, and Nora cuts her eyes at me.

I look down at the bell. "*S* is engraved on it!" I say to Ruqi. "Do you know what *S* is for? Ssssss-ssssss-snick—"

"Snickerdoodle!" she sounds out.

"Ruqi, where did you find this? In the bathroom?" I ask.

"Um . . . no . . ." Ruqi says.

"We didn't see this in the bathroom," Nora adds.

Ruqi spins around and then points. "Over there!"

In the distance, a mist of colorful lights surrounds moving walkways. A rainbow seems to dance on the ceiling above it, lighting up and going out, lighting up and going out, while the walls beam out pinks, purples, oranges, and yellows—the shades of sunset. The floors surrounding the flat escalators seem to be almost moving too, like a slow-moving river, reflecting back the dancing rainbows.

"Cooooool," I hear myself say like an awestruck kid who's never seen one of these walkways before. I have. Lots of times. Just not one like that.

"I mean, that could be a cool place for a cat," I say.

Hanna considers. "The movator? Did you find the bell there, Ruqi?"

"Ruqi could've gone anywhere in the airport when she went missing earlier. It can't hurt to look," I say.

"We're going farther away from our gates. What if Snicker-doodle isn't even there?" Sami asks.

"Well, we have to check out any and all leads, don't we?" Hanna says it more like a statement than a question.

Sami looks to Nora, whose face lights up as she swipes open NokNok on her phone, ready to post this wild light show.

"Maybe . . ." Sami whispers.

I try not to run, even as the dancing colors get wilder and bolder the nearer we get, and I can feel the others rushing behind me.

"Wait for me!" Ruqi calls, but I know the others got her.

Closer now, we gasp at what we see. The ceiling looks like a for-est canopy of thick green leaves with colorful tropical birds that light up in a repeating pattern. Nora squeals as she holds up her phone to capture it. I hear her talk to her followers, but I'm too focused on following the path of the pattern to listen to what she's saying.

We stop when we hear it.

"Was that—" Sami begins to ask my same question.

"It was!" Hanna and Nora exclaim together.

"Snickerdoodle!" Ruqi cries out. We all heard the shriek— a cat's shriek.

We dash onto the walkway, looking around frantically. I can't believe we're actually doing this. We're finding Lala Hoffa's cat! I picture myself shaking hands with Doc Hoffa. I picture myself on *Storm the Stage*!

But then, after a few moments, I notice Sami's face scrunch up in confusion. We're hearing other sounds. Bird sounds. Fake ones, coming from the forest leaves. One sound is almost like . . . the screeching of a cat.

"Ohhh," Nora says as we step off the walkway.

Hanna's face drops.

"That doesn't mean the cat isn't here. Ruqi found her collar bell!" I say, "Ruqi, where exactly did you see Snickerdoodle's bell?"

"Um, um . . ." Ruqi makes a face I've seen before—the one she makes when she's about to snitch a cookie because Mom isn't looking.

But Ruqi couldn't be lying. Why would she lie? Just to get on the movator? For a joyride? That joyride was sick! But still.

"Did you find Snickerdoodle's bell over here somewhere?" Hanna asks, still hopeful.

"Um . . ." Ruqi turns around and around. She's looking hard, like there is a place that she's trying to remember.

"Think, Ruqi," I urge.

"Over there!" Ruqi points across the hall to a subway-like silver train.

"The plane train, Ruqi?" I groan. Another joyride.

"Yes! There!" She jumps up and down.

"That goes to the international terminal," Sami says. "Ruqi couldn't have gone there and made it back on her own."

Honestly, though, knowing Ruqi, a part of me wonders if she could find her way back. Hanna looks like she's thinking it's possible too.

Nora crouches down to Ruqi's level. "Are you sure, habibti? Maybe it was just *close* to the plane train?"

That makes more sense. "Ruqi, you didn't get on the train, did you? You saw the cat go close?" I ask.

Ruqi is now pointing above. "In the ceiling! Snickerdoodle goed there!"

Nora and Sami exchange glances. Hanna's shoulders droop.

"I'm sorry, y'all. Sometimes, Ruqi makes things up," I explain, embarrassed. Ruqi never gets when something is important.

"Up there!" Ruqi yells again.

"Stop it, Ruqi," I grumble without looking at whatever ridiculous place she's pointing to.

"Feek, look!" Ruqi stomps. She stomps whenever she can't get her way. Because everything is about Ruqi getting her way. She's even making the cat search about her.

"You've taken us far enough. We're. Not. Going," I grit out.

I snatch her hand and head back to the movator, not caring whether the others are following. She twists, trying to get out of my grasp, even hitting my arm with her free hand.

When she points and says, "Look, look!" I am exasperated.

"Shut it, Ruqi!"

"It wouldn't kill you to be nice to your sister," Nora says.

"What? She's the one—" I look at Sami and Hanna, who look away. "I wasn't even mean—"

Ruqi points at me dramatically. "You mean!"

Nora takes Ruqi's hand and turns toward the train.

"Hey, wait up!" I yell.

Hanna's pocket meows, stopping all of us. She pulls out her phone—which meows two more times—and then she lets out a whoop.

Has Snickerdoodle been found?

I LOOK DOWN AT MY PHONE AND IMMEDIATELY DO A double take.

RainingCatsNDogs messaged me again! To respond to *my* message that our visit to Zoomi wasn't successful. And the notification preview says, NOT THE DOMESTIC ZOOMI . . . I click on it without a second to lose. "Whoa! Oh wow, oh wow, wow!"

"What?" Feek asks, tipping his head to try to get a look at my phone.

I turn it around so everyone can see. "It's from RainingCatsN-Dogs! We were in the wrong luggage store! Snickerdoodle was sighted in the Zoomi in the *international* terminal!"

I look at their faces and see that they don't get it. "We need to get on the plane train immediately! And get off at the international terminal! Let's go!"

Sami stiffens. He swivels from Feek to Nora before sputtering, "Nope! No! Not getting on that train! This is . . . it's a terrible idea! I'm not doing it!"

"Hmm, just because Snickerdoodle was spotted there doesn't mean we'll find her there now. That sighting was a few hours ago,"

Nora says, doubt clouding her face, "and we saw the domestic Zoomi store closing."

This is why you need people to be actual animal allies. It takes commitment to pursue justice for *all*.

I cross my arms, shake my head, and turn my voice quiet and serious because they still don't get it. "If we want to save Snickerdoodle, if we want to do the right thing, we need to get on that train. Even if there's just a small chance she's there, we have to check it out. She could be in serious danger."

I start walking toward the train terminal without checking to see if they're following me. Feek was the only one who looked like he was sort of considering it.

But it doesn't matter.

Because maybe I'll just have to do this whole Snickerdoodle rescue operation *all by myself.*

I DON'T KNOW IF WE'RE GOING TO FIND SNICKERDOODLE IN that Zoomi store, but I follow Hanna anyway. I posted a quick video of the collar and us on the movator with #SaveSnickerdoodle, and it's seriously the best thing that's happened to me all weekend. Not only did I get a bunch of new followers, but in the comments, Mackenzie and Kennedy were cheering me on. Sumaya even commented with praying hands and "hope you find her," which is really generous because she's angry with me.

Before I board, I hit record and give my followers a quick update. "Guys, we've had news of a Snickerdoodle sighting in the international terminal. I'm headed onto this plane train to check it out, so be sure to favorite me and get all my updates. This rescue mission is just getting started!"

CHAPTER 17

FEEK

I FOLLOW HANNA AND NORA TOWARD THE TRAIN, BUT THIS time instead of seeing another Ruqi joyride, I see the El train back in Philly and a younger Dad, who still had most of his hair under his kufi, standing in front of it. I'm suddenly small again. So small my hand disappears into my dad's as he pulls me onto the train so fast my feet can barely keep up.

Dad's jaw is tight. He's going to perform again. Back then, no one ever liked Dad's train performances except me. He steers me into a seat and moves to the aisle. He announces that he's going to share a poem. Like all the other times, people look away from him, look down at their phones like he's not even there. But this time, *this time*, a few seconds into the poem, something different happens.

A woman yells, "All right now!"

A few people snap.

"Tell it!" another man shouts.

People are looking and listening, enjoying my dad!

He says a line, loudly and boldly. People whoop and shout out at this one, clap their hands. The whole train is a mess of cheering, encouraging voices.

I jump to my feet and run to Dad.

"That's my daddy! That's my daddy! I'm with him!" I yell, jumping up and down. Some people laugh.

Dad's eyes, which had just been lit up, widen in shock. "Go sit down. You're ruining everything," he whispers harshly.

Yeah, I ruined my dad's first successful performance even if it was just on an El train. I wonder if he still sees me that way, as a silly kid who doesn't get it. A kid who gets in the way of special moments like Ruqi does. Maybe if I find the Hoffa cat, that would change? Dad would have to see me differently if Doc Hoffa rewarded me with an appearance on *Storm the Stage*. Would Doc let me?

"Watch, watch, watch! You have to watch her!" Sami interrupts my thoughts as I step onto the plane train. Ruqi is behind me.

"Sorry . . . it's . . . She almost went into the gap," Sami continues, pointing at the space between the platform and the train.

"Oh no! Ruqi! Sorry, I was recording," Nora says, rushing over from her spot on the train.

"She's fine," I say, irritation in my voice as Ruqi skips inside the car. "That gap is barely two inches. Ruqi is small, but not *that* small."

Nora looks, and I can tell she also sees it's far too narrow for Ruqi to get trapped in. She still rolls her eyes at me, though. Hanna, for her part, is typing furiously into her phone, not seeing any of this. Other than us, the train is completely empty. I guess with no planes taking off, there are no terminals to get to.

I stand in the doorway looking at Sami, who is still standing awkwardly on the platform.

"Are you coming in?" I ask, irritated.

"I . . ." He looks around, at the sky lounge across the hallway, at the potted plants to the left, like he's looking for a way to back out.

Suddenly, we see a woman in gray clothing and a dark vest with SECURITY emblazoned on it headed in our direction. Sami inhales sharply. "That Zoomi guy *did* say he was calling security . . . She's . . . coming straight for us?"

A robotically perfect woman's voice chimes, "Next stop, international terminal. Doors are closing."

We both look at the guard. *Is* she quickening her pace?

Sami almost knocks me over jumping into the train, and the doors slide shut.

After a couple of moments, Sami is still shaking. I feel bad for him and say, "We're fine. I'm sure she wasn't after us. That Zoomi guy just kicked us out. That's all. He didn't really call security."

He whispers something I can't hear.

"What?"

He speaks, and I still have to strain to hear it. "I said . . . maybe you should worry a little."

"What's that supposed to mean? It's good to stay calm and not worry," I say, a little louder than I mean to. Sami winces.

Nora says flatly, "Yes, don't worry about anything at all. Let your sister get lost in the airport. She'll be fine."

"I worry about her enough! I keep Ruqi safe!"

Sami looks at me for a split second, clearly confused, before catching himself and quickly looking away.

Nora chuckles at this.

"Just mind your business!" I bark at them.

Sami retreats to the corner of the train, where Ruqi is twirling and stumbling, and Nora barks back at me not to talk to her like that.

I look up at the train ceiling, ignoring Nora, who is *still* telling me off when the train begins slowing down. *Worry more? Like Sami? Nah.* Staying calm—staying sure that everything will be fine—is what makes everything work out. And everything will work out. We will find this cat.

The robotic female voice tells us, "Please step out for the international terminal."

Hanna finally looks up and grins. "We're here!"

CHAPTER 18

SAMI

WE'RE STILL IN THE AIRPORT.

It's not like we're in Siberia.

But as we spill into the international terminal, it feels like we've stumbled into totally different territory. I can tell from Feek's expression and Nora glancing around curiously that it's not just me. Beethoven, Bach, or Mozart—one of those folks—is playing low in the background, and there's a raised cathedral-type ceiling with gold and silver flowers etched in a geometric pattern. There are cushy sofas all over with people camped out, many of them sleeping, and—

"Are those trees?" I ask.

"Looks like it." Feek nods at the leafy not-fake-at-all trees planted in enormous multicolored pots all around this area.

The far wall is designed to look like a floor-to-ceiling window, but it's not a real window because it's daylight in there, and there's a rotating display of shimmering art overlaying it.

"So . . . now what?" Nora asks. She's got her phone in her hand.

"Now, we go there." Hanna points to the back wall lined with shops.

Following her gaze, I see a makeup store, a perfume shop, a watch store with a huge board advertising gold watches, and there it is—the Zoomi luggage shop. There's just one problem.

"They're closed," Feek says. "The luggage store is shut down."

He's right. Metal grates cover all the shop entrances, including the Zoomi store's.

"I told you it would be closed," Nora says. "It's almost nine thirty. Most retailers share the same hours."

Hanna's eyebrows furrow together. "Well, just because it's closed doesn't mean . . ."

Her voice trails off. Thunder rumbles in the distance. She crosses her arms. I feel bad she has to concede defeat, but I'm also relieved. We've officially reached a dead end. There's no way we're prying open the metal grates like Hanna is probably considering right now. We'll have this little adventure and head right back to our gates, and I can show my mother that I "made a friend" and Hanna can feel better because she tried her best. A win-win in a pretty lose-lose situation.

Just then, a door swings open in the distance, and someone exits.

"Whoa!" Hanna is no longer confused or flustered. She's smiling like she just spotted an enormous banana split with her name written all over it.

"Uh-oh," Nora says.

"The door!" Hanna says. "The one that he just came out of. That must be the corridor that the employees use."

Feek nods. "My cousin works at a clothing store in the mall. They have a hallway just for employees."

We hadn't noticed the door before, but now we can't unsee it. It's white with a white handle. Probably so it blends in with everything else. Probably so people won't notice it. Probably so annoying kids won't get ideas to go on an adventure . . .

"Hanna." I need to stop her. But it's too late. She's marching toward the door.

"Hanna!" Feek calls out. "Hold up!"

But Hanna is there now, and she's pulling at the door that very clearly says RESTRICTED: EMPLOYEES ONLY, but that, to my relief and Hanna's obvious disappointment, stays completely and absolutely shut. She puts a hand on her hips.

"There's got to be a way in," Hanna murmurs.

"Then what?" Nora asks her. "What would you want to do if you were able to get in?"

"It's a hallway," Hanna explains. "It'll lead to the back entrances for all the stores."

"You really think the cat's still in that luggage store?" Feek asks, his eyebrows raised. "That tip came in a while ago, right?"

"No, don't you understand?" Hanna says excitedly. "We're never going to find Snickerdoodle out here with all these people." She looks at the tired passengers in the distance and lowers her voice. "Cats want quiet. Especially a lost and terrified elderly kitty. Even if she's not in the Zoomi store, she's probably hiding somewhere back there." Hanna eyes the door wistfully and gives it another unsuccessful yank. "Getting in here is the key."

"The door is locked," Nora reminds her. "If you want, we could peek through the grates? We've come all this way. May as well check before we head back."

That sounds fair. I nod. And then we *do* need to get back. That's what I'm going to say. That we should get on the train. I'm feeling smug that my mom might realize shooing me away to hang out with a total stranger wasn't a great idea, but I *am* getting antsy about being so far from our gate.

I don't get a chance to say this. Before I can open my mouth, the handle turns, and the door parts. We hurry aside as a woman in a blue apron walks out with her clear plastic purse. She saunters toward the escalators. In a flash, Hanna sticks her foot out and blocks the door just before it can swing shut.

"Hanna." I stare at her. "What. Are. You. Doing."

She brings a finger to her lips. Looks straight at me. "Sometimes it's better to ask forgiveness than permission."

I OPEN THE HEAVY DOOR AND STEP INTO THE NARROW CINDER-
block corridor confidently, knowing that the rest of them will
follow if they see I know what I'm doing.

The back entrances to each of the closed stores are probably
in that hallway up ahead. Once we get there, we'll turn right and
find the one that opens into the Zoomi store—where, tucked into
some cozy nook, Snickerdoodle may be dreaming of her rescuers
bursting in at any moment.

I haven't figured out how we'll get *into* the store through a
locked door, but as my math teacher always says, every problem
needs to be solved in steps and only when you come to that step.

The step we are at right now is called Casing the Joint.

This joint—the corridor leading to the hallway behind the
stores—is narrow, with dim yellow light beaming down from the
ceiling. The floors are concrete, and the walls are made of big
white glossy bricks.

We just have to reach that hallway up ahead. And we're
in business.

And if Snickerdoodle is not there—she's got to be here
somewhere.

This is the perfect quiet space for a scared cat to want to hide.

"Um. Hanna." Feek's voice carries over my shoulder. I turn around and see he's stepped inside after me, but with one foot still out. "I'm all for finding this cat. Don't get me wrong. But it's probably a really big deal to walk through a locked door at an airport."

I start walking.

"Feek's right," says Nora, peering over Feek's shoulder. "I'm pretty sure there are laws against that kind of thing."

"Well, it was open, right? My brother's friend Zayneb—she's like my sister—tells me that sometimes when things are meant to be, doors just open, and look how easy it was for us to have access to this place!" I'm now in the hallway, which stretches in front of me for a dizzyingly long distance. I can't even see the end of it. But what I can see are doors spaced apart on the right side, the side we entered through.

The side that has stores facing out into the airport.

Bonanza. I point ahead. "Snickerdoodle is probably behind one of those doors."

When I say that, Ruqi scoots by Nora and runs through the corridor to catch up with me at the junction. Feek's other foot moves in, and Nora sighs and walks in too. Only Sami's feet remain firmly outside, but his head and shoulders stick all the way in. He looks shocked, and I immediately look away. Seeing his expression might make me worried about being here too, and the only thing I should be worried about right now is Snickerdoodle.

"You guys!" Sami hisses. "We can't break into places!"

"Sami, we're not breaking in!" I hiss back without looking at the half of his body that technically is "breaking in" too. "We are finding a lost cat!"

I start walking again before Sami can say anything else. Ruqi keeps pace at my side and Feek and Nora bring up the rear, their feet hurrying, like they want this done with.

I quicken my steps too.

A door slams shut behind us.

We all turn in slow motion.

Sami has stepped into the hallway too, and maybe he forgot how heavy that corridor door we all came through was, but he just let it shut behind him.

Uh-oh. I hope it isn't a self-locking door. Maybe one of us, maybe Sami, should have kept the door open a crack in case.

It's too late for that now.

Sami catches up to us, whispering, "I'm here to make sure you guys don't get yourselves into any more trouble."

We all walk quickly but quietly down the eerily silent hallway, Nora muttering the names of the stores she thinks we passed by. There are some hallways on our left, but we're concentrating on everything to the right of us because that's where all the stores are.

I silence my phone because Operation Rescue Snickerdoodle requires noiselessness, and there are presently twelve different meows set for a variety of notifications.

"I think the Zoomi store is going to be the next one, once we're past that other hallway," Feek whispers.

"I think so," I whisper back. "We should just—"

But as we're about to reach the hallway, a loud metallic sound clangs from it.

Then the sound of keys jangling.

Like we're inside some kind of superhero comic, all of us—even Ruqi—press ourselves flush against the wall and fall completely silent.

But I have to see. This could be it.

This could be another door opening, like Zayneb told me.

I crane my neck and peek into the hallway on our left, where the sound came from.

Yes, another door is open. I can't see whoever is there. The sound of keys clinking against one another continues.

Then, all of a sudden, the person steps out and, before I can pull my head back, I see a uniform like a person working in a hospital wears. Scrubs, I think they're called.

I risk another peek.

The person is walking away, their back to us, still going through keys. Suddenly, wisps of something I'd read somewhere comes to me: something about hospitals and animals and an airport in California.

Something bad. Sad.

Terrible, actually.

But I can't remember what it was.

I step forward quietly, and as the door the person in scrubs left from is about to shut—a door that says AUTHORIZED PERSONNEL ONLY in big red writing—I fold my fingers on the handle. And stop it from closing.

Then, like a ghost, I sidle inside.

It's dark in the small room, so I keep the door opened a crack but not wide enough for the person in scrubs to notice.

Just wide enough for a bit of light to spill in and reveal the truth.

When I see the needle-disposal container with a huge red skull sticker and the rows of medical equipment neatly arrayed on the shelf inside the small closet-like space, it all comes back to me—what I couldn't put my finger on before.

Being in this nightmare place, I remember what they did to traveling animals in that airport in California.

CHAPTER 20
FEEK

HOW DOES A PERSON GET THE NERVE TO JUST GO ANYWHERE at any time like Hanna does? Nora's jaw drops wide open. I look at Sami's bugged-out eyes, probably as bugged out as mine are right now. Are they right to be scared? All that stuff on the plane train that they said about me needing to worry more. Were they right?

I look at the door to the room Hanna's in. It's slightly open. It would be so easy to slide in and join her. I don't know if Sami is right, but what I do know is that Hanna is taking chances to do stuff that matters. So what if some things might go wrong? Isn't saving a life—even an animal's life—worth it? And especially if it's Doc Hoffa's cat? And saving that cat means possibly my biggest chance ever?

I look back. Nora is holding Ruqi's hand. Good, Ruqi will be okay. And she's been okay. I haven't left Ruqi in danger like Sami and Nora say.

I look at the door again. Take a breath and move to go toward it. That is, until I hear Nora gasp as Ruqi rushes toward the door herself.

"Ruqi?" I whisper-shout, reaching for her.

Ruqi swings the door open wide. Hanna stands in the center of the small room, and I see a look on her face I haven't seen before. Fear.

I move closer, and even from where I'm standing, what I can make out stops me cold. What is this place? It's like someone made a dark closet into a medical office from a horror flick. Long medical tools (For what? Surgery?) lie out on a little table. Are those restraints around the narrow bed? To strap someone down? Who are they for? And what is with the containers with skull labels? I move again to grab Ruqi and pull her out.

But, in an instant, I see Hanna, with a finger at her lips, pull the door almost shut, blocking my view of them, and I am snatched back against the wall. I feel Sami's hand shaking, still gripping my hoodie. He puts a finger from his other hand to his lips as we hear voices.

CHAPTER 21

SAMI

VOICES.

There are people. At least two.

They are steps away from us.

Over the pulsing beat of my heart, I try to listen to what they're saying.

"What are you still doing here?" a woman asks.

"Stayed late to wrap up some files. We had more cases come through than usual," the man replies. "Don't want to drive in *that* storm!" he says as a crack of thunder clangs muted in the distance. "How's your evening going?"

I look at Hanna and Ruqi as the two adults keep talking. The door to the supply closet is slightly ajar—their faces peek out at me. They're frozen in place. Waiting. We should leave. Now. But if Hanna and Ruqi hurry toward us, those adults might notice. What happens if we're caught? What's the consequence for sneaking into a restricted area? From the look on Hanna's and Ruqi's faces, it's clear they don't know the answer to that question either.

I'll peek out. Just the tiniest bit. Glance into the hallway ahead of me so we can see where the adults are, so we can help Ruqi and Hanna get out of that supply closet without being seen. Before I can move, the man speaks, and what he says sends a chill down my spine.

"He seriously sent *another* email on the whole thing?" The man sighs. "I am sick and tired of hearing his opinion about that cat situation."

That. Cat.

As in *our* cat?

As in Snickerdoodle?

"Seriously!" the woman exclaims. "Just because he's the head of PR, he thinks he can send anything he wants to. His opinion isn't the only one that counts."

"Alfred's squeamish about the articles. Lost cats make for bad press."

They're definitely talking about Snickerdoodle. My mouth is dry, like I've swallowed sand. They're close by. Whoever they are, they are close enough for us to hear without having to strain our ears. How are Hanna and Ruqi going to run back and join us without getting caught?

I glance at Nora—she's pressed against the wall—before looking at Feek. He looks more scared than he did when I first met him and he was looking for Ruqi.

I need to be strong for him. I'll just peek out. See where those two voices are coming from. Really quickly. Maybe they're farther away than I think—sound probably carries fast with the cinderblock walls here. If so, I can wave Hanna and Ruqi over. We can make a break for the door we came in from. Before I can take a single step, the woman speaks again.

"He can send all the emails he wants—it's not going away just because we pretend it's not happening. You know, Jake from the Zoomi store texted me a little bit ago. He was approached by a group today," the woman says. "These were just a bunch of kids. But we're getting calls every other day about animal disappearances. It's like a second job now just fielding them."

My shoulders hunch up to my ears. Us. They're talking about us. And did she say animal *disappearances*? As in plural? As in more than just Snickerdoodle? Just how many animals are lost in this airport? Feek's jaw is dropped open with surprise. Nora's recording, but her hands are shaking.

"They're trying to play Nancy Drew to kill time between flights," the man says. "I'm always tense lately, waiting for someone to back me in a corner to interrogate me. I work at the clinic— why would I even know anything about it? It's like when that cockatoo got out three months ago."

"I'm trying to block that out completely," the woman groans. "The owner bought tickets for flights just to get past the TSA and harassed *everyone*. Between that app where everyone's trying to catch make-believe animals and the real-life animals running loose, I'm over it."

"Well, I wrote back to Alfred," the man says. "Told him I back security's position. We have to get rid of the animals."

"Thank you," she says. "The more of us saying so, the better."

Wait. What? *Get rid of the animals?*

"Maybe if enough of us get involved they'll finally bring down the hammer and get rid of this *whole* animal headache once and for all," he says.

"It's been done before. I don't know why they're acting so squeamish."

"Right," the man says. "Like the airport in California. Let me know if I can help with getting that across to them."

"Just let me know who's trying to make waves. They've got to be squashed right away."

Every word they say is more terrifying than the last. Hammer? Getting rid of animals? Squash them?! Squash who? *Us?* And . . . what happened in California?

I look across the hallway. Hanna looks like she's going to be sick. So does Feek. And Nora. And me? I'm scared I might just barf right here and now. This is even bigger than Snickerdoodle. It's a conspiracy! They're getting *rid of them? And squashing whoever gets in their way?*

"We have to get out of here," I whisper.

"Not without my sister we're not," Feek whispers loudly. Too loudly. His voice is shaky. "I have to get her. I'm not risking them getting to her first!"

I look at Hanna and Ruqi in the slightly open supply closet. Even though the space is not well lit, I can see Hanna's face has gone pale.

Calm down, I tell myself. I want to fall into a puddle on the floor, but Coach Madea talks about this all the time in competitions—how it's normal to be afraid. We don't have to push away the fear, because doing that just makes the fear roar louder. Instead, we greet the fear and let it sit with us while we take a deep breath and get on with what we need to do. I've only ever done that in my competitions, but that's what I have to do here. And this is way more important than any karate competition. I won't let any of us get squashed.

I inch closer to the edge of the corridor. I peek out. Phew. They're not as close as I thought. They're ten feet away. Maybe more. Their backs are to us. For now.

I wave my hands frantically to Hanna and Ruqi. Urging them to come.

"What are you doing?" Feek hisses.

"They're not looking this way," I whisper back. "This could be our best chance."

Feek bites his lip. Then he gestures to Ruqi too.

Slowly the door parts more. Hanna and Ruqi tiptoe out. The door closes silently behind them. Good. They're moving toward us. Feek nods encouragingly, his hand urging them to keep going. Ruqi is being so brave as she grips Hanna's hand tightly.

They're almost here. Almost . . .

And then they're here. Relief floods my system. We're all together. And now we'll go. But before any of us can make a move toward the door, we hear a deep voice.

"What are you doing back here?"

The man in scrubs. The woman, in an all-black uniform with SECURITY emblazoned in yellow above her right shirt pocket. With handcuffs dangling from her belt. And a gun. Their arms are folded. They're not smiling. And they're staring straight at us.

I NOW GET WHAT PEOPLE MEAN WHEN THEY SAY THEIR blood ran cold. The moment I see that bald man and the guard woman with the tight bun towering above us, I feel a shiver go right through me, like my body is circulating ice. What is really going on at this airport?

My hands were shaking so much, but I went live on Nok-Nok and captured everything. We've got loads of witnesses, and this makes me brave. No matter what we've done, it's nothing compared to what these employees are doing. *Getting rid of them. Bringing down the hammer. Squash them.*

Just let them try and squash me. They don't know who my mom is. She'll squash them right back!

I lock eyes with Sami, Feek, and Hanna so they'll know I got this. I stand up tall and find Congressmom's take-charge voice and say, "What does it look like we're doing? We're trying to find the bathroom."

Sami, Feek, and Hanna nod enthusiastically to back me up. Maybe a little too enthusiastically because the man in scrubs and the security woman aren't buying it.

"Young lady, you better not be recording. This is a restricted employee-only area."

I shove my phone in my pocket but leave it on so at least the audio will record.

"Nope, just looking at my airport app to find the bathroom."

The security woman points toward the door. "Out."

The man in scrubs and the security woman move toward us while making shooing gestures. It's actually very rude, if you ask me.

"We're going. We're going," Feek says.

"Yeah," Sami says. "You guys really sh-should get better signs for the bathrooms."

"Really, yeah," Hanna agrees. "You need better signs."

By now we've made it to the door with the guard at our backs. She ushers us out and then points rather emphatically to the obvious sign for the men's and women's bathrooms.

"Do you kids want to tell me what you were doing before or after I call your parents?" she says, standing so close to me that I can read the name B. White on her name tag. Her arms are folded. She taps her foot. The man in scrubs is just behind her, with hands on his hips, waiting for our answer.

I feel cold-afraid all over again. I search for some legitimate reason why we went in the wrong door, but it's as if my mind has lost all its words.

I hear Hanna say, "Well, you see—"

"Yeah," Feek chimes in to save her, "you see—"

"You see—" Sami says to rescue Feek.

And then it hits me to RUN. R-U-N. RUN!

I grab Ruqi's hand and take off, sprinting. The rest of them don't need instructions to follow, and they take off too. From behind us, I hear the guard radio, "This is White. I've got five kids, trespassing in an employee-only area, on the run."

CHAPTER 23

FEEK

BALDY GIVES CHASE

Bunhead wanna race
Train fly out the space
Gone without a trace
Who's scared? Who's rattled?
Cat slayers, we'll battle
Run 'em out the place
Their turn to skee-daddle

CHAPTER 24

NORA

SAMI IS ALREADY AT THE TRAIN, LEANING AGAINST THE DOOR frame, holding it open. Ruqi is still clinging to Feek's neck when they cross the threshold. Hanna rushes in next, and I follow shortly after. As soon as we're all seated and accounted for, Sami finds a place to sit too.

I grab my phone out of my purse. I'm panting, but I manage to say, "You guys heard everything. There's something shady happening to animals at Hurston Airport."

I put my phone away and catch my breath. I can't believe our small group of five kids just outran security. We barely knew each other a few hours ago, and now we're on this incredible mission together.

When the doors slide closed, it's the sweetest beep I've ever heard. All I wanted was to get away from my mom, but now I can't get back to her fast enough.

THIS IS HUGE. THIS GOES BEYOND SNICKERDOODLE.

This is about animals at airports everywhere.

I get my phone out of my pocket.

There are three missed calls from Dad. And a bunch of unread messages. The one on top says, "WHERE ARE YOU? I NEED TO TALK TO YOU" but I'm not going to check the rest.

I need to get to my notes app ASAP.

Besides writing down everything we saw and heard in that corridor, I need to reread and take notes on what went down in California, in the airport that was all over the news a year ago due to another lost pet.

My notes will be needed when we talk to someone high up here at Hurston.

I'm about to type the ominous phrase "Get Rid of Them" as the title for my notes when I catch a glimpse of Ruqi's eyes. They're still and full of fear as she rests her head on Feek's shoulder. He moves his hand and lays it on her arm, like he's consoling her. Then he gently eases the unicorn headband off her head and places it in her hands, closing her fingers around it. She hugs it to her chest, and her eyelids begin to shut slowly, her head still leaning against Feek.

In the seat behind them, Sami looks scared too. He stares ahead and then blinks rapidly in turns.

He's processing.

I lower my phone.

I realize this is huge for another reason. We just uncovered something really scary, something that involves people who actually work at the airport, like store employees, doctors, and security.

Something only we know.

The five of us working together got to the bottom of this case.

We need to do this part together too. The part where we help each other understand what's happening.

I led them on this investigation, so I need to lead them now as well.

We're the only ones in this train car, so we can speak freely. "Are you guys okay?"

Sami angles forward and checks on Ruqi. "Is she sleeping?" he asks quietly.

Feek nods.

Sami sits back. Then, his eyebrows scrunching with worry, he speaks. "Hanna, what happened in California? What were they talking about?"

I lean forward. "In the San Marzino Airport, they were tranquilizing flying pets without their owners' permission."

"So they weren't *killing* them?" Sami asks, shuddering. "They said *get rid of them,* so I thought . . ."

"Well, they might not have *meant* to kill the animals, they just wanted them to be easier to handle. But one died, a parakeet named Victor." I let that sink in.

Everyone is quiet, absorbing this awful information.

And then I get a sudden realization.

What would make a cat run away? Most cats?

A visit to the vet. Someone coming toward them in a lab coat and mask with a needle pointing up.

"I wonder if Snickerdoodle was trying to get away from being tranquilized here at Hurston," I whisper. "Remember one of those cruel people said, *They should just do what they did at that airport in California?*"

"Oh my God," Nora breathes out.

"Ya Allah," Feek says, shaking his head.

"We have to make sure they don't get away with this," Sami says. "But . . . do you think they're going to come after us? We . . . we know too much, don't we?"

"They have nothing on us," Feek says. "Except that we went into a hallway we weren't supposed to."

"And, don't worry, I've got it recorded that they're the ones who are in on some plan to get rid of airport animals. So if there's anyone who should be getting in trouble, it's them," says Nora.

"Yeah," Sami says, "and I bet your mom knows someone in charge of airports who can help us. You know, someone in the Federal Aviation Administration."

Nora nods with confidence. "That's right. The truth will come out, and we all saw and heard the same thing, so there's lots of witnesses."

Feek straightens himself and adjusts Ruqi's head at his side. "But they'll still say we're just kids."

"Well, too bad for them, because kids change the world too," I say, sitting up. "All the time."

Feek looks at me. "Yeah, that's true. And we got proof."

"Exactly. And you're right, Hanna." Nora flashes me a smile. "*We* can change the world. I'm sharing it right now with all these new followers I got on NokNok." She taps on her screen and says, "I've got like a couple hundred more people here."

Sami looks over at me and Nora.

The fear is almost all gone from his eyes.

There's something else there, something new, but I can't put a finger on the emotion.

He sits back in his seat, watching the station stops flash on the map above the car doors, and it hits me what I see growing in his eyes now.

It's pride.

Sami is proud to be a part of this team that's doing the right— *and brave*—thing.

We're going to save Snickerdoodle and break this thing wide open!

RUQI WAKES UP AS SOON AS THE PLANE TRAIN STOPS. FEEK is the first one out the door, holding Ruqi's hand. Sami exits next and scopes out a place for us to discuss our next move. He motions for us to join him behind a row of tall plants.

"We should go straight to my gate and talk to my mom," I say.

Hanna looks up from typing into her phone. "You're probably right. With these guards after us, we'll need your mom to get us in touch with the people in charge."

Ruqi lets go of Feek's hand and looks through the plants. Feek hisses at her to stand back, but she will not move.

"I see Cookie Cat," she says.

I peer through the plants at the sky lounge for Jet Atlantic, a sleek storefront with tall, frosted-glass windows. I've actually been in these lounges before, at other airports, back when my mom had loads of miles from Jet Atlantic and we'd get upgraded. They're amazing. They have TVs, showers, free snacks, and hot and cold drinks. I used to love making hot chocolate and pretending I was drinking coffee.

But I don't see a cat. I'm about to tell Ruqi she might have been mistaken when Sami points and says, "Guys, wait, what was that?"

As soon as he says it, we all see it. First, the shadow of a fuzzy tail. Then, as it creeps closer, the outline of a cat, moving across the window, and a person in what looks like a uniform, grabbing the cat while its back arches in distress.

"That's—Snickerdoodle. Isn't it?" he adds.

"It was definitely a cat," says Feek.

Hanna lowers her phone and stares at the silhouette.

"We have to go in there," Sami says.

I do a double take. Is Sami really suggesting that we do this?

He picks up on my disbelief and continues, "I'd much rather march straight to Nora's mom, but what if that was security who grabbed her?"

"But how do we get in there?" Feek asks. He glances around and lowers his voice. "There are people looking for us, *people who want to squash us.* And don't you have to be flying first class to get in?"

When Feek says that, it's like the lights switch on in my brain, and I say, "Wait! I have my mom's membership card in my wallet."

"Why does your mom let you carry around her card?" Feek asks.

"Because it's expired," I say. "I collect hotel keys and cards from places we've visited. It helps me remember the stuff I've done, like a scrapbook. My mom was going to throw it out, so I took it."

Feek shakes his head before adding, "It's a nice idea, but you can't go in there with an expired card."

"I probably can," I say while unclipping one of my gold hoop earrings and sliding it into my purse, "if I say I lost my earring in there while using the showers, and I beg the desk attendant to let me look super, super quick, and then I look around for the cat we just saw."

Ruqi jumps up and down to show she likes my idea and slides a hand into mine. "I'll come with you!"

My heart melts. I wish I had a little sister, and I can't understand why Feek wouldn't love always having someone who is ready to go along with anything he suggests. But that also makes it extra hard for me to say, "I wish you could, but you have to stay out here and help the other kids. We all know you have the best eye for spotting Snickerdoodle."

Hanna says, "Thanks, Nora. We have to check it out."

"So let's do this!" I say, excited to get back on NokNok Live with #SaveSnickerdoodle. Everyone loves a pet rescue, and this could rocket me so far past Mackenzie's and Kennedy's follower counts that there will be no more competition between us.

As soon as Feek and Sami give me a reluctant okay, I grab my phone and this handy device I keep in my purse for when I need to record hands-free. It goes around my neck and looks ridiculous, but it's totally worth it for this kind of footage.

When Feek sees me setting up my phone, he frowns. "Hold on. Are you going to record in there?"

"Of course," I say. "I have a lot of new followers on NokNok. One of them may have a lead for us."

This idea interests Hanna. "Nora's right. The video could be helpful to share with Animal Allies."

I turn to Feek and say, "See, I told you."

I hear my snarky tone and add in a more mature voice, "Everyone thinks NokNok is about getting attention for yourself, but when used well, it's really about reaching people. This is kind of like my job. I'm actually working here."

Sami shakes his head. "Nora, I know NokNok might be helpful, but this is serious. You don't want to get distracted and—the stakes are really high."

"I know what I'm doing, Sami."

"But—"

I bring a finger to my lips to motion for him to be quiet while I hit record and get my followers up to speed. "Hey, guys, so I'm still at Hurston Airport, searching for Snickerdoodle. My team and I think we may have spotted her inside this sky lounge, so I'm going to use a missing-earring ploy to sneak in and have a look around. Pay close attention to my audio because I won't be in full focus, but if you see Snickerdoodle or have any news of her whereabouts, be sure to say so in the comments and use #SaveSnickerdoodle."

I duck out from behind the plants. When I approach the sliding doors, I turn back and give the group a thumbs-up. Feek looks exasperated and Sami looks worried, but Hanna gives me a grateful smile that warms my heart. She appreciates me taking this cause to a wider audience, and that is what my work on NokNok is all about.

I take a deep breath and head in. At the long, wood-paneled Jet Atlantic desk, an attendant about my mom's age is standing behind the counter in a starched navy-blue uniform.

I flash my card and hope she doesn't stop me.

But I'm not that lucky.

"May I help you?" she asks.

"Oh, yes, please," I say in my sweetest talking-to-adults voice. I read her name tag and add, "Ms. Carol, I was in here with my mom, and we used the showers, but I think I lost my earring back there."

I pull my hair behind my ear to reveal my bare earlobe.

Carol's brow furrows. Before she can ask me any questions, I fold my hands together and plead, "Please, I don't have a lot of time. They were my grandmother's earrings, and my mom is going to be so sad if she finds out I lost one. Is it okay if I go back there and look?"

Her lips knot together. She's about to say no.

"I'm so stressed about my mom finding out," I add. "I won't touch anything, and I'll be super quick."

Carol sighs and says, "Hold on. Let me see if anything was brought to our lost and found."

My heart races. I'm actually pulling this off! I must be a really good actress.

She pulls open a drawer and peers inside. "Honey, there's nothing here. How about if I take your number, and I'll let you know if we find anything."

That's my cue to bring out Extra-Dramatic Nora. The key is to become so emotional that the other person can't ignore you. Extra-Dramatic Nora always works on Congressmom, especially when we're in public.

First, I make my bottom lip quiver, and then I carry all that shaky, nervous energy into my voice and say, "I know you can't leave your desk, but I'll be real quick. I promise. I wouldn't ask if it wasn't such a precious family heirloom."

When she sighs, I know I've won her over. "I can't allow you to wander around without an adult," she says while reaching for a BE BACK IN FIVE MINUTES sign. She props it on the counter and says, "So we'll have to be quicker than quick, okay?"

I clasp my hands together. "Oh my goodness, thank you, thank you."

I pivot and wave frantically in front of the glass to give the other kids a signal to come in. I hope they see it. With Carol escorting me to the bathroom, it's going to be up to them to get inside and look around.

Carol gives me a puzzled look. "Everything all right, dear?"

"I just saw the biggest moth. Don't you hate moths? I hate moths."

She shakes her head and motions for me to follow her. I have to work myself back into her good graces, so as we walk, I say, "Thank you again for helping me out. I'm always losing things, and it takes a real toll on my mom. Do you have kids who are as irresponsible as me?"

She laughs and says she has a daughter my age and that, yes, she's prone to misplacing things too.

Bingo! "You know, my mom is always telling me if I want to wear special family jewelry, I have to be more careful," I say, "and I really am learning that valuable lesson today. That's why she even makes me wear my phone around my neck. My mom says I'll lose anything if it's not attached to me."

Carol smiles as if she's had the same thought about her daughter, and I take that as a sign that I've made a solid connection. When she asks me which shower stall I used, I point to the last one in a row of four. This will buy me at least a couple more seconds.

The other guys better have figured out a way to get in by now.

CHAPTER 27

FEEK

WHEN NORA GIVES US TWO FRANTIC WAVES, IT'S PRETTY clear that things aren't going according to plan. Ruqi is about to bust through the door.

As gently as I can, I say, "Wait, Ruqi. We have to figure out how to do this so we don't get Nora in trouble. Then, we can find Cookie's ca—I mean, Snickerdoodle."

"But how?" Sami asks. "We can't just go in and look."

I sigh. He's right. Everyone will know we're not supposed to be in there.

"Can we distract them? So we can look?" Hanna asks.

"Four kids walking into a sky lounge is the distraction. There's no way these people won't notice us," Sami says. His shoulders wilt.

"We can't just give up," I tell them. And then, something Dad always says just hops out of my mouth: "When something is hard, you don't just give up. You stand tall and show up. Time to show up."

Ruqi squeals, "Showtime!" the way random people on the subway sometimes do. Suddenly, I have our distraction.

"Showtime!" I exclaim with a laugh. Sami and Hanna look at me like I've lost my mind. "They'll look *away* from us. I know what to do. There's a kind of show people do on the train back in Philly. I've seen it in New York too. Everyone looks away, especially if it's bad. I'll handle everything. Just follow my lead!" I don't tell them that I purposely do watch these subway shows to make the performers feel better. I'm so energized I almost skip through the door.

Sami stares wide-eyed and whispers, "A show? This. Is. Bananas."

"You saw Snickerdoodle," I say. "It's either save her or whatever cat that was or leave them in danger because we're too scared to do the right thing." I take a breath and repeat, "Follow my lead."

I puff out my chest, grab Ruqi's hand, and walk through the sliding doors of the sky lounge like I'm supposed to be there. I look around the carpeted, high-ceilinged room, with plush leather chairs shaped like fancy boxes—boxes filled with people. I see from the walls of windows that the storm is still raging wild as ever. I swallow. So many people. A few look up at me and I nod calmly. Finally, I spot it: a coffee bar, with foam cups. I beeline to it, grab a couple, and give one each to Hanna and Sami, who look at me confusedly.

Can I do this?

When I see a flash of lightning out the window, something sparks in me, and I pull Ruqi to the front of the crowded room. Before I can change my mind, I yell, "WHAT TIME IS IT?"

Ruqi, without missing a beat, hollers with me, "SHOWTIME!"

A few heads immediately look down and away from us when I shout this. They know the deal.

"Yes, it's showtime, folks! And have we . . . um . . . has the Jet Atlantic sky lounge got a show for you! Please show us how much you appreciate it! With tips! Twenty dollars? Fifty dollars? One hundred? We know you folks got it, and we know you want to give it!" I smile when everyone who was still looking up becomes suddenly busy with their phones.

"Let's go!" I motion to Sami and Hanna, who start wandering around the room with their cups, their eyes darting everywhere. I look around too, but there's no cat.

"Hey, I don't think you're allowed to do this in here," a man in a three-piece suit says. "This is the sky lounge."

I make sure my voice is calm when I say, "It's a new policy, for entertainment purposes."

"New policy?"

"Yes, you can read it on the sky lounge website. Click on the About tab, then click on the Guest Services link, then hover your mouse over the Arts and Culture button until Entertainment and Celebrations pops up, double-click that, or maybe it's a right click or a left click, then scroll to the paragraph that's third from the bottom of the page."

When I'm sure he's sufficiently confused, I start to beatbox, except I of course don't know how to and sound terrible. Spit is flying out of my mouth. I act like I don't care.

"Help me out, Ruqi!" I yell, and somehow she is worse than me. Our beats don't even match.

"Y'all feel that?" I exclaim like it's the best thing ever. Hanna and Sami for their part are doing a good job searching while holding out their cups like they're really collecting money.

I start to rap, "I'm the words to the song . . ." but then I realize, *no, this has to be bad.* So, I say,

"I'm the words to the song
Bom bibbity bom
These rhymes go hard, they go deep deep
Boopity-boppity-beep-beep
I'm the farmer in the dell
Hear me yell
E-I-E-I-OOOOOOOOO
YOOOOOOOOOOO!
Eenie-meenie-miney-mo!
Give up your money, yo!
Dum diddy dum diddy dum
You got the money! Give us some!
Rat-a-tat-tat, rat-a-tat-tat
There was an old cat
Who ate an old rat"

"By the way, have you guys seen any cats around here?" I ask the crowd. But I've done too good a job and no one will even look at me.

I'm running out of bad rhymes, and Hanna and Sami still haven't searched the whole room. I wonder about Nora for a second. How is she keeping that attendant in the bathroom?

"ARE YOU SURE, HONEY?" CAROL ASKS WHILE PULLING BACK the curtain. "This stall is dry, and it has an OUT OF ORDER sign on the showerhead."

"Oh, really?" I say, pretending to be surprised. "They all look the same to me. It's so confusing. Maybe it was this one?" I point to the next shower, and we both peer in. But there is no earring on the ground, of course.

"I should step inside to be sure. The gold kind of blends in with this tile."

She gives me a dubious look, and I wonder if I've taken things too far. With her hands on her hips, she says, "Honey, the tile is white. If it was here, we would see it."

"Hmm," I say with a finger on my chin.

This gesture may have been too over-the-top for even Extra-Dramatic Nora, and Carol makes a disapproving tsk before saying, "Now when did you say that you were in here? Lots of people have used these showers today with all the flights being grounded. Someone might have taken it, or it might've already gone down the drain."

"Let me try the next stall to be extra sure," I say.

I take my time, looking up and down each wall, to which she says, "It's an earring, dear. It can't stick on the walls. Come on, let's take down your name and number, and if anyone finds it, we'll call you."

I nod and say, "Okay, thank you, but I'm just going to try the toilet stalls first. I used the bathroom, and maybe it fell off there."

She sighs loudly and says, "Fine, but hurry. I can't be away from my desk much longer."

I repeat thank-you and add, "I'll be so quick," even though I know I'm going to be so slow. I just hope I'm slow enough to give the rest of the group time to find what we're really looking for.

"COME UP OFF THAT MONEY, Y'ALL!" I YELL. "WE GOT DANCE moves too!" I start wildly doing a running man, an old dance my parents like to do to crack each other up. Ruqi giggles and does it with me. Even Hanna is jigging as she works her side of the room. And Sami . . . I'm not sure what is happening with Sami. Is he okay? He's rocking from side to side like he's dizzy. You know things are serious when even Sami is trying to dance. At least, I think that's what's happening.

I look toward the back of the room where the bathrooms are. Still no Nora and attendant yet. Good. The room is huge, but we're almost done. Just a few more rows to go. I break out the moonwalk. *Hurry, Sami and Hanna!*

I KNOW FINDING SNICKERDOODLE IS MY NUMBER-ONE MISSION
in life right now but . . . is . . . Sami . . . *dancing?*

Is that what someone would call the way his body is moving
like a pendulum of a cuckoo clock while his arms jiggle up and
down? And his face grimaces and then attempts to smile all relaxed and then grimaces again?

Maybe in a dictionary it would be classified as dancing, my brother
Adam's voice enters my head. *But not in the actual world we live in,
where rhythm must be involved for it to be pronounced "dancing."*

But when Adam said that, he hadn't been talking about Sami's
dancing. He'd been talking about Mom's.

Because she'd sort of danced like Sami. Though her dancing
was not tentative like his, but prouder, with more energy in her
pendulum movements. And her face had always been full of joy
when she danced.

Or so I've been told.

I wasn't there.

I shake my head free of Adam's voice and Mom's dancing and
focus on the task: to find out if Snickerdoodle is actually in the
sky lounge.

It's hitting me: *Sami*'s the one who wanted to come inside.

Feek is performing.

And Nora went undercover. *For Snickerdoodle.*

They're all now completely in on the mission!

I'd better do the best job I can looking around. "E-I-E-I-OOOOOOOOO!" I sing along to the refrain of Feek's pretty awful yodeling-rap. I'm trying really hard to keep my first impression of him as Very Cool, but when he started singing, I found myself wondering if he was Actually Cool—in real life, back at home and at school, I mean.

"They say the cat in the hat is all that. But where you've been at?" Feek raps, and the crowd is trying hard not to groan unanimously, which is perfect because they're also concentrating on ignoring us unanimously. It takes my all to continue sticking my cup out like I really mean for these snobby people to fork over cash for this "talent"—though *no one* has put even a penny in. (Mental note: rich people are not generous.)

(Or maybe they've just got good taste in rap.)

Sami glances over at me mid-grimace and shakes his head. I shake my head to indicate I also see no cat, but then start nodding back encouragingly for his dancing, and swaying as though I'm following his rhythm, weaving in and out of rows. Marking each row's end is an electric-blue side table with a tall cylindrical glass vase full of blue marbles. I counted six vases I've made my way around so, between Sami and me, we should be done soon.

I add some arm movements to my swaying, a few NokNok moves this crowd of serious-looking adults will probably not know, as I continue dancing between the seats, scanning for any evidence.

Remembering Nora might come out of the bathroom at any moment, I quicken my pace, but then, two feline eyes stop me.

There's a cat staring at me from inside a sleek black carrying case with wire grating at the front, back, and top. The cat carrier, labeled MICHELANGELO, sits on a chair beside the cat's adult.

Michelangelo is the most beautiful, well-groomed fluffball in two shades of brown, with a golden bell on his collar and all-knowing green eyes.

I bend down to say hi, and he blinks lazily yet enchantingly. His adult looks up at me for a sliver of a moment and then goes back to her phone.

There's a sticker that says ONBOARD: SEAT ALLOCATED on top of Michelangelo's carrier.

"Oh, that's nice," I say, approvingly. "Michelangelo's getting a seat on your flight."

The adult nods without looking up from her device.

"Only some airlines allow that, so I'm happy for Michelangelo." I can't help adding, "I wish all airlines were so kind, don't you?"

The adult, a lady in a plaid dress with tall lace-up boots I would definitely wear, says, "You seem to really like cats."

"Yes! All animals. Equally. Speaking of which . . ." I lean forward and whisper, "Have you seen a cat around here? The one that went missing at the airport a week ago? Snickerdoodle?"

The adult shakes her head. "The only cat I've seen is the other one in the lounge. She's over there. She has anxiety, so the owner takes her out of the carrier every so often."

I turn to where she points.

Another cat carrier. This one is hot pink. The door to it is open, and the cat is nowhere around.

Aw. She's in the corner, near a vase of blue marbles, being cuddled by a tall man in a suit who's murmuring things to her.

Why can't all animals be treated so preciously?

Why are only some privileged to be privileged?

Why can't every being be treasured for being?

I want to hug all the sad, lost animals like the tall man is hugging his cat, an all-white long-hair.

Which is *not* Snickerdoodle, a dusty-white Himalayan.

She . . . is . . . not . . . here.

She's somewhere scared and worried about the future, all by herself, missing her mother—I mean, her parents, her family.

I glance around the sky lounge. Feek is still freestyling. Sami is still swaying like he's in a trance while he works his way down the last row opposite me. People are still looking away.

Nora will be out any second now.

I finish scanning my last row and then dance my way to Sami. "E-I-E-I-OOOOOOOOO!"

"I met a dog over there," Sami whispers. "No cat, though."

"I saw a cat in the corner with that man in the suit. It's probably the one we saw through the window. But she's not Snickerdoodle, and she's actually in good hands," I assure him. "Now we have to leave here real smooth before Nora comes out. Keep up the dancing until the last second, the crowd is totally buying it. I'll give Feek a signal—"

Uh-oh. When I tell Sami to keep dancing, he suddenly gets extra energized, and his arms shoot out in weird spasms and, like I'm seeing it in slow motion, a nightmare unfolds: Sami tips back, his arms flailing, and HE KNOCKS OVER A VASE, A TALL VASE, FULL OF BLUE MARBLES!

THERE ARE GLASS SHARDS.

And blue marbles.

Everywhere.

I look around at the crowd—it's silent. People in the lounge are looking at me.

All of them.

Are looking.

At me.

Because I did it. I broke the vase. One extra step, and BAM.

Heat rises to my face. I need to do something. I need to break out of the petrified state I find myself in and get a broom. Clean up. Fix this.

"What are you all *doing* here? Really?" A woman with a laptop narrows her eyes and studies me like I'm an invading alien.

"That's right," the man next to her says. He holds up his phone. "I checked the website. There's nothing on there about this. It *does* say the sky lounge is meant to be dignified and businesslike." He straightens his tie. "Which means *you all* have no business here."

"We, uh—" Feek begins. But the man cuts him off.

"Where are your parents? Where's the attendant? I swear, kids these days." He takes a step toward the counter. "She's got to be—ahhhhhhh!"

His foot steps right onto a pile of unfortunately placed marbles. His eyes widen as he slips backward, his arms flailing wildly before he lands flat on his back among a field of blue spheres. The woman with the laptop gasps. Setting it aside, she rushes over to help him up. The attendant is rushing toward us. Nora is close behind.

"Oh my God. Oh my God." The attendant gasps as she surveys the chaos. Her ponytail has come loose; stray tendrils of hair frame her face as she looks around frantically. "What *happened?*"

She turns, and her eyes lock straight onto mine. She studies Feek and Hanna and Ruqi. "What are you all doing in here?"

"I'm—I'm so sorry," I stammer. "This was my fault."

"We can explain," Hanna says.

For the first time in my life I wonder: How securely are eyeballs glued in a person's head? Because hers really look like they might fall out.

"Out!" she sputters. "Now!"

"I'm sorry, miss," I tell her. "Please let me help clean this up. I can pay for the vase and—"

With pursed lips, she points to the sliding door. "Now, or I'm calling security."

That gets me moving. We hurry out, careful to avoid the stray marbles still rolling across the tiled floor. I should be relieved that we won't be in trouble after all. But will *she* be in trouble now? I can't believe all this happened because of me taking one wrong step.

I guess it's not *that* hard to believe.

"That was a pretty awesome performance," Nora says once we're in the hallway, across from the lounge. "What I caught of it, anyway."

"If by pretty awesome, you mean pretty awesomely awful, then yeah." Feek puffs his chest out and grins.

"But no Snickerdoodle," Hanna sighs.

"Well, at least we ruled it out," Feek says.

"And it was fun!" Ruqi chimes in.

Fun? Someone slipped and fell because of me. I broke a vase! And—my heart pounds—Snickerdoodle is *still* lost out there. She is still in danger.

"Hey, it's okay. Accidents happen." Hanna looks at me like she can read my mind. "But now we have to go to Nora's mom before we get caught. Congresswoman Najjar will know what to do next."

And we'll be safe there, I hope. Nora's mom won't let anything happen to us.

"It wasn't completely pointless." Nora stares at her phone as we hurry down the hallway toward our gates. Her pace slows, and her eyes go wide. "Look." She holds it up to us. "I've got like a hundred new followers!"

We all look at her. Hanna blinks.

"That's great that you have even more new followers," Feek says in a flat voice. He keeps glancing back. I follow his gaze. No one is behind us. Not yet.

She glares at him. "That's not what I meant! I mean—yeah, that's cool, but they're sharing with #SaveSnickerdoodle! Like I said, the more people that share, the more leads we could get! And, wow, people really care about this. They're tagging all kinds of animal rights groups to amplify this story . . ."

"Good!" Hanna says as we hurry along. "And—"

But her words cut off when a beeping noise fills the hallway. And then—the loudspeaker crackles on.

CHAPTER 32

ANNOUNCEMENT

"PAGING TAUFEEK STILES, RUQAYYAH STILES, HANNA CHEN, SAMI IQBAL, AND NORA NAJJAR. PLEASE REPORT TO THE SECURITY DESK AT TERMINAL ONE. PLEASE REPORT TO THE SECURITY DESK AT TERMINAL ONE."

Zora Neale Hurston Airport

Case Notes – Hanna A. Chen

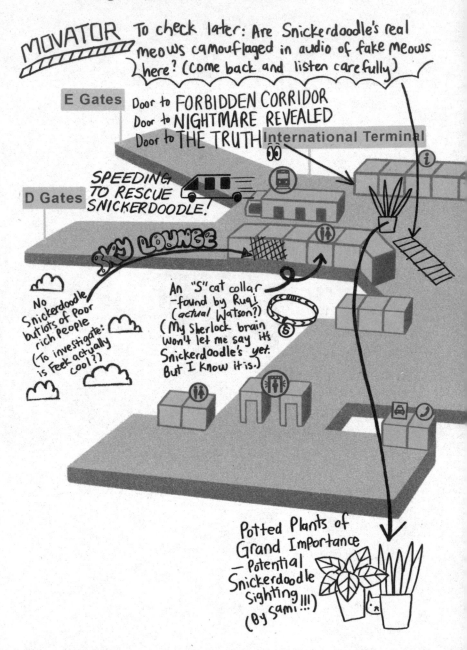

MOVATOR To check later: Are Snickerdoodle's real meows camouflaged in audio of fake meows here? (Come back and listen carefully)

E Gates

Door to FORBIDDEN CORRIDOR
Door to NIGHTMARE REVEALED
Door to THE TRUTH International Terminal

SPEEDING TO RESCUE SNICKERDOODLE!

D Gates

SKY LOUNGE

No Snickerdoodle but lots of poor rich people (To investigate: is Feek actually cool?)

An "S" cat collar – found by Ruqi (actual Watson?) (My Sherlock brain won't let me say it's Snickerdoodle's yet. But I know it is.)

Potted Plants of Grand Importance – potential Snickerdoodle sighting!!! (by Sami...!)

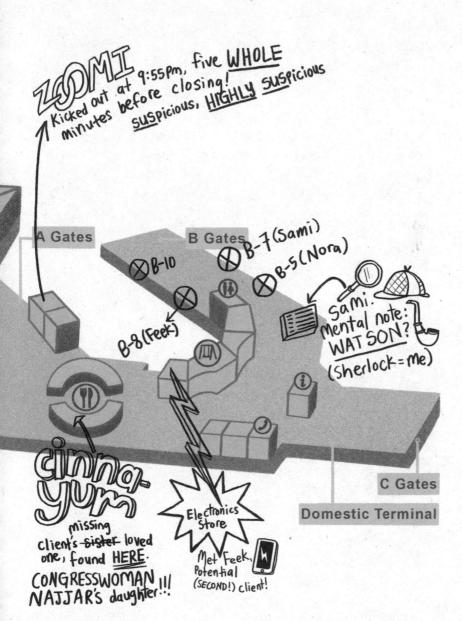

ZOOMI
Kicked out at 9:55pm, five WHOLE minutes before closing! SUSPicious, HIGHLY SUSPicious

A Gates

B Gates

B-7 (Sami)

B-5 (Nora)

⊗ B-10

⊗

B-8 (Feek)

Sami.
Mental note:
WAT SON?
(Sherlock = me)

cinna-yum
missing
client's ~~sister~~ loved one, found HERE.
CONGRESSWOMAN NAJJAR'S daughter!!!

Electronics Store

Met Feek,
Potential
(SECOND!) client!

C Gates

Domestic Terminal

FUGITIVES.

One second I was feeling nervous. Scared. But also fired up. The way I do right before a karate match—the way I was in the corridor earlier today—nothing scaredy-cat about *that* Sami. Even though I was terrified inside, it was like I was on the brink of saving the world. At least, the world of airport pets. We were going to talk to Nora's mother. We were going to tell everyone what was happening at Hurston Airport and save the day. And the next minute, the announcement blares through the speakers overhead, stating in no uncertain terms that we are wanted. I'm going to puke. The reality of what is happening is settling in:

We're not *just* wanted. We're fugitives.

I first read that word in a book last year. It was the chapter title, and for approximately two seconds, I thought the word meant a type of fudge and I got all excited. It had to be a gooey, fudgy-wonderland type of dessert with a name like that. But then I read what my teacher calls "the context clues" around it—a man on the run after robbing a bank—and my definition clearly didn't fit.

But *fugitive* fits here. Because that's what I am. That's what all of us are. Fugitives. We are on the run. I glance at Ruqi and stifle a sob. Even four-year-old Ruqi is a fugitive right now. My heart's beating so fast I'm actually terrified it might explode, and there's no bathroom to splash water on my face to calm me down. Even if we are on the side of what is right, even if we're doing this because we don't want to get squashed, it doesn't mean it isn't terrifying. And no one better tell me I'm overreacting now. As we hurry down the hallway, it feels like the walls are closing in on me.

Looking around, this is the first time we all look the same level of terrified. We know way too much.

We need to reach our parents and the higher-ups here as soon as possible. Nora's mom will help us. She'll protect us when we whistleblow this major operation. We're turning the corner toward our gate when I see them.

Security guards.

The lady we saw in the corridor. And three other people are with her. Some with gleaming handcuffs hanging off their waists. All staring at us with unsmiling expressions.

I feel dizzy. Whatever is about to happen . . . it's going to be bad.

Very, very bad.

CHAPTER 34

FEEK

I ALMOST RUN AGAIN. BUT AS I TAKE IN BUNHEAD, ONE TALL man dressed up in a professional gray suit, and two other guards in blue uniforms, I know we can't get away. I exchange glances with Sami, Nora, and Hanna and see that they know it too.

One of the uniformed guards says, all serious, "Come with us," like we're criminals. And it makes me remember, we're not the ones who are criminals here, and we've got the evidence to prove it.

I say, "Yeah, okay," and give them an I-don't-care smug look. The guards exchange glances.

"Kids are so bold nowadays," one of them says.

"They'll try to stop us from speaking to the press," Hanna whispers.

"It's like this hadeeth my dad likes to say," I tell her, saying it loud enough for these four stooges to hear. "If you see evil, change it with your hand, and if you can't, do it with your tongue, and if you can't, hate it in your heart, but that's the weakest. We can't let them get away with this."

"Are you serious?" Sami grits out, stopping abruptly when he sees the guards turn to eye him. Ruqi is still hanging onto me, her arms around my neck, and we both crash into him. He stammers out a "sorry" then lowers his voice to say, "Hanna's right, though. You really think anyone's going to admit what they're doing here? We're kids. How will anyone believe us?" He whimpers a little. "What will our parents do? We're going to be in so much trouble."

I blink a few times. He can't be right. Can he?

I shiver at the thought of my mom knowing even half the stuff we've done tonight.

"Of course we're in trouble. Hello! We just uncovered a crime," Nora says. "My mom will understand when I explain it to her. She'll know how to fix this. Plus, I recorded everything, so it's all there in their own words."

Hanna's eyes light up at this. "Congresswoman Najjar will know exactly what to do!"

I smile at that until I hear a—oh no!—baby crying. Is that Hamza's cry?

We round the final bend to the security desk and there they are:

A man dressed like Sami, who is talking with another man, who is staring at his shoes and folding his arms (or maybe hugging himself?). A woman who has the same scared-face look Sami sometimes gets. She's holding and trying to calm a baby. I zoom in on the blanket. She's calming Hamza! I look behind her and see my mom, her eyes wild and the congresswoman calmly patting her shoulder.

Even from back here, I can hear the congresswoman saying, "Breathe, Halima, breathe" to my mom.

Mom looks up, and her eyes lock onto mine.

"See, there they are, perfectly fine," the congresswoman says aloud.

"Sami!" says the man with grown-up Sami clothes.

Mom takes Hamza from the scared-faced woman. "Thank you, Yasmine. I think he's just going to fuss until he falls out from exhaustion," she tries to joke, but I hear Mom's voice and know better.

The woman—Sami's mom, I figure—runs over to Sami with his dad.

Sami is silent.

The self-hugging man opens his arms and almost runs to Hanna.

"Dad . . . I'm okay," she says. She looks around him, concerned, then focuses on Bunhead, who has taken a seat at the security desk. Bunhead looks back at Hanna with an anger that makes my breath catch.

"Please get the paperwork started, Officer White. We'll need to file a report," Gray Suit tells Bunhead. I feel a chill.

Ruqi jumps down from my arms and runs to Mom. Nora and I follow after her. Mom's eyes lock onto mine again. They make me feel her pain. Feel her hurt.

"See, the children are fine," I hear Congresswoman Najjar repeat. "What matters is that everyone's safe and sound." She now pats Nora's shoulder.

Standing in front of Mom, I see tears in her eyes, and I feel like the worst son that ever existed.

"Why . . . How . . . How could you?" she asks.

"I'm sorry, Mom." My voice cracks like I might cry too. I want to explain what's happening to the animals and that this is for Doc Hoffa and Cookie, but my voice is gone.

Mom grabs Ruqi's hand and turns on her heel without another word. But before we can go anywhere, Gray Suit storms over to us, gripping a walkie-talkie. The same anger on Officer White's face is mirrored on his.

"WE'RE GLAD YOU'RE HERE," I SAY QUICKLY, BEFORE THE MAN in the gray suit can get a word out. "We need to talk to someone high up in security." I hitch my fingers in the straps of my backpack, my voice firm but low. I'm trying my hardest to make sure Dad doesn't hear too much.

The woman with the bun, B. White, has her arms crossed hard, and the man in the gray suit has a stern face.

"I *am* the head of security," says the man—Bruce Rock, according to his name tag. "And you all are in some serious trouble . . . Several sky lounge passengers complained about you sneaking in to disrupt the peace. *And* you entered a restricted area of the airport."

"Like we said, Sami would never do such a thing," his father says, taking a step forward. "Sami, tell them yourself."

"Um." Sami's face is growing redder and redder by the minute.

"Sami?" Sami's mom exclaims, her face aghast.

Uh-oh. I have to shift the narrative. "We know all about what you're doing to the poor pets at this airport!" I say.

"What I'm doing to who?" Bruce Rock draws himself up to his full height, which is very high, his fingers holding his belt loops.

"Not you, sir, but the airport. It's the same thing that happened at San Marzino Airport in California. Tranquilizing animals before they fly! Without permission! We saw the needles and the tranquilizing liquid! We saw the tranquilizing room! And the evil doctor!" I'm speaking loudly but quickly because I've become aware that while Feek, Nora, and Sami are looking intently at Bruce Rock to see his reaction, all the adults are staring at *me*, and not in a good way. I'm *this* close to being pulled away—by Dad, and, worst-case scenario, by all the parents working together. But I'm also *this* close to cracking the case! "And we know that's what happened to Snickerdoodle here! But she got away!"

"That . . . that's right," says Feek, clearing his throat. "I saw it myself. And your security guard here, B. White, is part of it. She was talking to the doctor about getting rid of all the animals."

• "I heard it too," says Nora. "In fact, I have it all recorded."

Nora pulls out her phone and turns up the volume. But there's only muffled sounds, garbled voices, thundering footsteps, and a video that is too blurry and shaky to make out anything. "Oh no, oh no, oh no, oh no—you guys, I just looked at the comments, and lots of people are just saying that they couldn't hear or make out anything."

"Wait. How—" Feek sputters.

"It doesn't matter! They won't get away—" I draw myself up to look Bruce Rock right in the eyes. "*You* won't get away with this!"

"Now listen, how is it that you kids, who broke several laws in this airport, are telling me off right now?" Bruce Rock says, his face scary as it looks down at me from very high. It hits me that Bruce Rock is very big and might possibly be related to The Rock, the actor.

"I didn't say *you* did something wrong, Mr. Bruce."

"No, but you kids *did* do something wrong. You went into a restricted area of the airport. You could very well be charged with trespassing."

"Mr. Rock, Congresswoman Sarah Najjar here," Nora's mother quickly interjects, putting out her hand to shake Bruce Rock's. "We are so sorry for what happened. With the flights being canceled and all the stress, I think the kids got bored. You know how kids can get when they're antsy. It's a new situation. You've got to understand."

We are sorry? I stare at Congresswoman Najjar.

She thinks we were running around because we were bored?

"Please." Congresswoman Najjar smiles and continues with her appeal to Bruce Rock when he doesn't respond. "I'm sure they've learned their lesson. And will be very careful of breaking any laws henceforth. And be mindful citizens. Which is a win for all!"

Bruce Rock shakes his head. "No one goes anywhere until I've had a chance to review the security footage again. There's plenty of time, but even if flights resume, no one is boarding until you get the all clear. I suggest you all go back to your gates now."

Congresswoman Najjar doesn't lose a beat, the smile still on her face. "I hardly think that's necessary. The sooner we get these kids home and out of a cooped-up airport, the better for everyone. We'll have them under our close supervision until we leave, and I am absolutely certain that this is the last you'll hear from these children. Again, they are very sorry."

Bruce studies her and us. Then, "I'm sorry, ma'am. We need to review everything, and we need your information."

Congresswoman Najjar's face falls. Dad pulls out his wallet and walks to hand his identification over to B. White at the desk. Sami's parents are already there, waiting on whatever B. White is doing with their "information." Feek's mom is standing off to the side, soothing baby Hamza while she waits her turn.

I can't believe it.

They're all falling in line.

And I know Congresswoman Najjar said what she did to try to get us out of trouble.

But this is IMPORTANT TROUBLE.

"Pets are passengers too! They have rights like us!" I say, some of my anger at Congresswoman Najjar *apologizing* on our behalf bursting out of me. "What about all those poor tranquilized animals who just wanted to fly in peace with their families?!"

Bruce Rock stares at me and then forms a small smile. "What's your name, young lady?"

"Hanna. Hanna Chen, Animal Allies International member." I nod at the others. "And these are fellow concerned citizens."

Nora and Feek nod back at me. Sami just whimpers from behind them.

Maybe Bruce Rock is going to help us now that we're calmer.

Maybe we can now solve this like adults.

"Well, Hanna Chen, Animal Allies International member, what you're describing is *not* happening to any animals here or at any other airports that I know of."

"But San Marzino—"

"Hanna, stop, and come away right now," Dad says from behind me.

"The San Marzino Airport was a made-up story fueled by a tabloid that is currently in court being sued for fanning untruths."

"Victor died. Victor the parakeet!"

"Not from being tranquilized. Do your research, Hanna." Bruce Rock shakes his head and sighs like he's disappointed in me.

"But we saw and heard—" I start, but then Dad says, "I said, that's enough, Hanna!"

I turn to Dad, in shock at his voice.

What is happening?

"That area you all saw with the needles and medicine was actually the back of the airport medical clinic. The evil doctor you saw was a lab technician. And B. White right here is Security Officer Betty White, animal lover, who would never harm any pet. She's actually petitioning for animals not to be allowed to fly out of here until they make it more pet safe."

B. White turns her phone around to me. It's the Animal Allies forum, and in the corner it shows her AA name: GoldenGirl. "I want Hurston to cancel animals traveling until we have a foolproof way for them to fly safely and securely, like us humans do. Like Laxton Airport did in California."

I look up at her, and although she doesn't soften her face, I see her eyes. They are . . . *kind*. And, gulp, I see that the key chain sticking out of her pocket is of the panda from the World Wildlife Fund.

Bruce Rock suddenly smiles at me, and I can't tell if it's in a kind way or in an amused way. "Now, don't get me wrong. I'm happy you're so worried. I'm worried about that poor cat too. I want her found. And I love when kids care about the world. You're trying to do good, all of you." He nods at Feek, Nora, and Sami and then gives me another mysterious smile. "But remember: go out there armed with the truth. And you'll get more people onboard."

He turns around and follows B. White.

And everyone turns around and follows their parents.

But I'm afraid to turn around and follow Dad.

MOM IS ALL SMILES WHEN WE'RE AROUND EVERYONE ELSE'S parents. She comforts the moms by patting their hands or putting an arm around their shoulders. She checks in with the dads and says things like:

"All that matters is that everyone was found."

"Look at these budding young activists. One day they'll use all that imagination to change the world."

But as soon as we are out of earshot, her exasperation shows. She massages her temples and says, "Nora, what were you thinking? I was sitting there, working, and when I looked up, I saw all these worried parents from MONA gathered together. So I went over there, thinking I was helping them, only to find out these were the parents of the kids you wandered off with. And then we spoke to security, only for security to tell us you kids had been trespassing all over the airport! If the press gets ahold of this story, they'll spin it into how a bunch of Muslim kids got caught in an airport security breach and how one of them was the congresswoman's daughter. They'll make it sound like I was using you kids to plot some terrible scheme."

A bunch of Muslim kids? I slow down behind Mom as we walk back to our gate. Is she saying that the press will lump me in with these Muslim kids, or does she see our family as Muslim?

Even when I was running around the airport, I saw myself as me, Nora, and they were the MONA kids. I don't get how any of this works. Like, what does it take to be one of the Muslim kids? I don't know the stuff they know, the prayers they say when they're together.

And, honestly, I don't care right now. My whole world is crumbling. One minute I'm using NokNok to find Snickerdoodle. Everyone is sharing, and I feel like I'm saving the world. The next minute, I'm playing back a video that didn't record clearly, and my comments are full of accusations that I'm a faker. As if I had no real leads and I was using Snickerdoodle's search to get attention.

Even Kennedy and Mackenzie commented with skulls and shocked-face emojis. What does that mean? But the worst was seeing Sumaya's message. "First the birthday party. Now this. You're such a liar."

Maybe Sumaya's right.

I was totally wrong about all of it. Maybe there is a cat named Snickerdoodle missing somewhere in this airport, but that's just it. She's missing, and there's no big scandal we're uncovering.

Back at the security desk, I made it sound like I was only sad about not getting the evidence we needed so I wouldn't break down in front of everyone. But I'm SO embarrassed. I'm not even excited about having a ton of new followers anymore, because more followers are more people who witnessed this low point in my life.

I want to delete my NokNok account and hide forever.

By now Mom's a few steps ahead of me. Her sturdy, low-heel pumps click loudly against the floor, and I fall farther and farther behind. I can't believe I got in trouble with my mom, airport security, and the Internet all in one day.

I look around to catch a glimpse of the other kids. Hanna is walking off with her dad. I can't find Feek and Ruqi. They must be back at their gate already. And Sami's parents are giving him a hug.

Unbelievable. My life is pretty much over, and Sami is getting a hug. I bet his parents are asking him how all this is making him feel.

"Nora." Mom turns around to see where I am. She stops and waits for me to catch up before saying, "Were you listening? I'm explaining that airports are secured places, and what you did was illegal. I know it would be a nightmare to lose a pet like this. You were probably thinking about how you'd feel if you lost Gucci, but our family is too high-profile for you to risk getting in this kind of trouble."

Ugh. I broke the law and blew up my entire social life on NokNok, and apparently Mom thinks I did it all for my love of Gucci!

My cheeks flush with a hot mix of embarrassment and anger, and it doesn't help that while Mom is talking to me, she's also looking at her phone. Probably checking her messages to see if anyone has found out about this.

Mom's right. The press will probably find out because they always find out about everything, and that means even more people will know about this disaster.

I follow Mom the rest of the way to our gate, but I can't shake feeling stupid, not just for hanging out with these kids I don't know and will probably never see again but for posting about it too.

At the gate, the seats we had earlier in the day are taken, and floor space is limited with so many people sprawled out, trying to sleep. Mom's irritation grows by the minute as she scans our gate for a place to set up camp. She wrinkles her forehead and purses her lips. Then she sighs loudly and says, "I need to find an outlet. I've got to make some calls before things get out of hand."

It feels like another dig. She may as well have said, "I've got to make some calls to cover up your big mess."

Mom motions with her head for me to follow her to a space on the window ledge. It's wide enough for both of us, but I don't want to sit on a cold metal frame with nothing to lean against.

"I'll just sit here on the floor," I say, pointing to a large pillar with an electrical outlet at its base.

"Oh, good," Mom says, "you can watch our stuff while we charge. And Nora, no more wandering off. All of you kids need to stay at your gate until we leave. If any of those kids come over here again, send them back to their parents, okay?"

I nod, but I can't believe Mom is letting me sit by myself so easily. Mom should insist that I sit next to her and explain why all this happened so I can spill out everything about Kennedy, Mackenzie, Sumaya, and NokNok. She should keep asking me to talk even if I say I don't want to talk because, as the kid, I can't want to talk to her more than she wants to talk to me. It's like a rule or a law or something.

I slide down against the pillar. I'm afraid to pull out my phone, but I can't resist the urge to know what people are saying. Maybe it's not all terrible. I take a deep breath and scroll through the comments. This time, between the accusations that I staged our search, I see people rooting for us to find Snickerdoodle, people who believe in us. There's even a message from the Hoffmans.

Thank you, kids, for trying to bring our Snickerdoodle home.

It makes me think of Congressmom. When I get upset about the mean things people say about her online, she tells me, "Nora, I am elected by the people, but I work in service of causes. As long as I am making progress toward those causes, it doesn't matter what people say or think about me."

That's what Hanna tried to get us to do today. Serve a cause.

I sit up tall, hit record, and say, "Guys, I know some of you think I was faking my search, but I only wanted to help find Snickerdoodle. I'm sorry it didn't work."

I post the clip, and then I pull up my chat with Sumaya. I type something and then erase it. I type another thing and erase that too. There's no point. After lying to her about my party, she's not going to believe that I was telling the truth about looking for Snickerdoodle.

CHAPTER 37

SAMI

ONE SECOND PASSES.

Then two.

Three.

Thirty full seconds pass. No one speaks.

My parents face me as raindrops pelt the ground through the darkened window behind them. They haven't said a word since I walked back with them to our gate. My mom hugged me when she first saw me at security, but now they're just studying me, their hands on their hips. It's got to have been a minute by now. Which might not sound like a lot, but it *feels* like forever. Especially when no one's saying anything.

I wonder if I broke their brains.

"Sami." My father finally clears his throat. A whoosh of air buzzes from the vent above us, mussing his hair. "That was . . . It was . . . unexpected."

This gives my mother a jolt. Quickly nodding, she adds, "That's right. Sneaking into a *locked* facility at the *airport*? The whole sky lounge thing they told us about? How did this happen?"

"I told them they had the wrong kid," my dad says. "It couldn't be Sami. Not our Sami. Do you have anything to say to us?"

I look at my shoes. Silence stretches between us. I should answer them. Say something. A million different feelings pulse through me. I clench my palms. My whole body feels like it's rumbling. It's a new feeling. Like I'm a volcano on the verge of erupting.

"Sami," my mother says. "How did this happen?"

I jerk my head up. Is she serious right now? She is. She's looking at me with worried eyes and pretending she has no idea.

Just like that, molten lava erupts.

"How did this happen?" I repeat. "How. Did. This. Happen?" I swallow and then— "What happened is"—my voice rising—"I wanted to sit right *here* at our gate. I wanted to figure out how to get home. And *you* told me to go off with Hanna."

"Sami—" my mother begins, but I don't let her continue. I don't care if my voice is way higher than it probably should be and that the lady next to us isn't even pretending to not be eavesdropping but just plain old staring at us with wide eyes.

"I didn't want to go! I looked at you, Mom! You saw me shaking my head. You know I didn't want to go. Why would I EVER want to go off like that? But no." I throw up my hands. "You wanted me to get out of here because you were sick of me. You were sick of me freaking out. You wanted me to go away."

"Sami, that's not—" my father begins.

"My new *friend*," I interrupt. "That's what you called her, Mom. I talked to her for like five minutes earlier when I was checking flight times. You shoved me off to go and wander the airport with her. A stranger! I shouldn't have gotten on the plane train, okay? We shouldn't have been in that hallway. Or the sky lounge. I know that. But I didn't WANT to BE THERE in the first place!"

My mother's eyes water. My father's jaw opens and closes.

I'm pretty sure this is the opposite of how this is supposed to go. I was caught trespassing at an airport. They should be going off on *me* and telling me I'm grounded until I'm eighteen. But my parents? They're staring at me like I grew an extra head. Antlers too. I guess it's because I've never spoken to them like this in my life.

The lava stops flowing. I'm suddenly so tired. So tired my legs feel like they might just buckle underneath me.

My father clears his throat, but before he can say anything, I speak. "I know you have a lot to say"—my voice trembles—"but I can't right now. I just need a minute. Okay?"

I sink into the empty seat behind me. I pull out my headphones and plug them into my phone. I pretend I'm listening to music instead of the words going round and round in my head. The words I *didn't* say to my parents: *I'm sorry that even when I'm trying to help, I just make things worse. I'm sorry I'm not cool and confident like Ibrahim. I'm sorry you got your perfect son right away and now you're stuck with me.*

I CAN'T BELIEVE I WAS WRONG. SO VERY WRONG.

About so many things.

And nowhere close to finding Snickerdoodle.

I keep a gap between me and Dad as we walk back to our gate, but he moves closer and closer. Finally, as we near our seats, he puts a hand on my shoulder, and I almost jolt when I feel it.

It's firm. And strong.

"Hanna. Stop," he commands. "Let's move over there. People are sleeping near our seats, and we need to talk."

Dad lets go of me, and I stop but don't turn in his direction. When I don't hear anything more from him, I sidle my eyes to the side to see why.

He's moved near an information board and is waiting there with his arms crossed, staring straight at me.

Uh-oh. Dad's not supposed to get mad *at me*. I'm the one who has a right to be mad at *him*. He's the one who broke my trust. And went behind my back. To change our family.

I eye my seat. Maybe I could just sit down and ignore Dad completely.

Across from my gate, I see a sad sight. Sami's arms are crossed, and his parents are towering over him with frowny faces. I turn to check if I can see Nora. Maybe she's getting patted on the back by *her* mother because Nora's done a heroic thing, searching for a missing animal.

But instead I'm met with another awful sight: Nora's mom is marching ahead of her, talking and shaking her head while Nora follows, a dejected look on her face, her arms crossed exactly like Sami's.

"Hanna Amelia Chen, over here. Right. Now."

Stunned, I pivot to Dad's loud voice, a voice he doesn't use often with me—maybe like twice in his life before.

As if I'm not in charge of my body, I walk over.

And, again, like I'm not in charge of my actions, though I try my hardest not to look at him, my eyes rise to his face.

I feel compelled to check how angry he is.

His eyes flash. "No more. That's it. This is going to stop. Now."

He's angry. Really angry.

"We're done. This game. Completely done."

I lower my eyes and feel my shoulders hunching. The little words coming out of his mouth feel like stones raining on my head.

"This is not about a cat. This is about you trying to avoid me."

Even though that's not true—it *is* about a cat!—I don't say anything.

Because, yes, it's also about avoiding Dad.

"I've been trying to talk to you all weekend. And here at this airport. And you're running away, going as far as even getting in trouble with security!" His voice gets louder, and I close my eyes. "All this to not talk to your own father?"

I shake my head. *Doesn't Dad get it? I want to find Snickerdoodle. And it happened to be at the best time, when Dad wants to ruin my life.*

He doesn't get it because I can't open my mouth to tell him all that.

Because if I do, I know I'll cry so much they'll need to bring a mop to our gate, and who wants to see all that anyway?

I still don't open my eyes. They feel hot, and I'm pretty sure tears are rushing over to cool the heat.

I try not to squish my eyelids because that will just make the tears fall. Trying not to cry makes me take a sudden breath in and swallow, but still I sob when I let the breath out.

Dad lowers himself and puts a hand on my arm, and this time it's not the grippy kind.

I keep myself as still and quiet and closed as possible.

"Don't be so upset," he says softly. "I'm doing this for you, Hanna. For us."

My eyes fly open. *This? How is getting married to someone for US?*

No. He will not make me feel bad for being mad!

I turn to leave . . . but, UGH, there it is again. Dad's holding me. Tight.

"You are not going anywhere, young lady. We are going to go back to our seats. Maybe I can't make you talk, but I will make you stay right next to me."

As I turn to follow him, I glance around to check if anyone else can see this embarrassing situation.

And I see an even worse thing: Feek's mom is giving it to him, hands on her hips like Nora's mom, while Feek keeps trying to open his mouth, his hands moving with empty motions, sadness written all over his face.

Feek, Nora, Sami. All in trouble with their parents because of *me*.

Maybe Dad sees Feek because, with his hand still gripping my arm, he adds, "And don't try anything else, because you're grounded."

AIRPORT CHAIRS ARE DUMB HARD. BY THE TIME WE RETURNED
to our gate, our cots had been snatched and were long gone. Mom
and Ruqi are snoozing at my feet on some coats beside Hamza's
car seat. Somehow, I "lucked out" and got this unbending chair
with metal spikes for armrests that I can't sleep in.

So instead I try to do something that calms me. I write. Reread my unfinished poems. So many of them. The one from this
morning still pulls at me.

I'm the words to the song.

I read it, but I flash back to how Mom rushed back to the gate
earlier, Hamza rocking in her arms, Ruqi beside her tripping to
keep up, and me following behind.

All the way, she'd spat out how disappointed she was in me. How
I was grounded forever. How I needed to learn to act like an older
brother. How she'd had to go on a hunt to find Hanna's dad, hoping
maybe we were together. And how then they had to go hunting for
Sami's parents when Hanna's dad remembered her going to Sami,
and then the congresswoman got involved and then they got security, only to find we were in trouble with security. She tells me how

she couldn't believe I took my sister and the other kids to chase after a cat. How I had been so thoughtless and childish. *Childish?* Me?

The hammer to the gong . . .

And I see the look on Mom's face when she realized our cots were gone. It rocks me.

I am the beat to this rhythm—

"I have nothing left in me," Mom had said as she threw our coats on the floor and pointed to the empty chair for me. I hear it again and again in my head. *I have nothing left.*

I flip the page and rewrite a different poem.

Dear Dad,
Do lines drop down incomplete for you too?
Do your rhymes forget the beat, 'cause mine do?
Do you read your stuff and pray for better?
Do you go back? Cross out every letter?
Do you go back? Erase each mistake?
How do I erase a bad choice that I make?
How do I make someone know what I've known?
That I'm worth your time now that I've grown?
That I'm more than the dumb things I have done?
That your childish kid is now a dope son?

I groan and draw a big X over the whole page. I can't ask my dad these dumb questions.

•••

I don't know when or how I fall asleep, but I know what wakes me up . . . it's the same thing that wakes up the scowling people sitting next to me: Ruqi.

Her deep-throated snores, like an idling tractor trailer, rumble through the small, crowded space. People's heads shoot up from the floor and nearby chairs. Yeah, she is *that* loud. At home, Mom, Dad, and I joke about how someone so small can make so much noise. At home, it cracks us up when she sleeps like a dead person and is impossible to wake. But here and now . . . Mom and I aren't laughing. I look up at the large digital clock on the wall: 2:20 A.M.

Mom looks wide-eyed at Hamza, who, somehow still sleeping, squirms in his car seat, and I can see her mentally calculating whether Hamza could continue sleeping through this noise.

Ruqi lets out a sound that is somehow a roar and a snort at the same time, and Hamza whimpers. We lock eyes, and Mom begins to rock the car seat.

"I got Ruqi," I whisper even though I don't have a plan.

I look around. See the Rube Goldberg machine shining brightly in the open hall and point.

Mom shakes her head. But Ruqi snort-roars again, and Mom, panicking, whispers, "Okay, okay, okay!"

I stoop and gently lift Ruqi (who somehow weighs more, knocked out) along with her coat and carefully walk to the big glass fixture in the hall, gleaming in the darkness. I carefully lay her down on the floor and sit against the machine beside her. It's turned off, but I hear a sudden scary creaking sound from inside it. It stops just as suddenly, and I shrug—must be rusty gears. Ruqi snort-roars on. I give up on any thoughts of sleep.

CHAPTER 40

SAMI

IT'S 2:45 A.M., AND MOM AND DAD ARE KNOCKED OUT. THEIR heads rest against each other, their mouths are slightly parted, and my dad is snoring so loudly, you'd think there was a grizzly bear on the loose in addition to a missing cat. This would ordinarily be mortifying, but there are currently plenty of snores floating around the airport.

Me? I've never been up this late, but I'm awake like it's the middle of the day. Which is a good thing because there is a *lot* to do.

Maybe it's because there are a lot fewer people using it, but the Wi-Fi is finally up and running. I take advantage of it to get to work. I emailed Jerome the list of moves I was planning to use for the competition—Coach Madea will probably pick him to replace me since he was my practice partner. I forwarded Jax the videos I'd downloaded with singalong parts for the drive up. And now I pull up my notes app on my tablet and type out the rest of my to-do list for when it's polite enough to call people like Ms. Babs, our neighbor, who'll need to pop in one last time to check on our rabbits and make sure they have water and food. Though I look out the dark airport windows and feel a slight bit of hope. It's still raining pretty hard, but it hasn't thundered in at least an hour. I won't be going to the competition either way, but it'll be nice to put this airport behind me. *Call Coach Madea,* I type in. Once it's late enough to make phone calls, I'll borrow my mom's phone and tell him about my flight. It's kind of weird—I've been so worried about missing the competition, staring at the departure times until my eyes went fuzzy. But now that it's happening—I'm officially missing the bus ride, the competition, everything—and I'm not even crying. If I can't be there, I'll do what I can to help my team from here. Before I can finish typing my list, an alert pops up: Battery low.

Seriously?

I groan and rise up. Craning my neck, I scan the walls for an outlet. But every single port is in use. Most of the people curled around their charging devices are fast asleep. Now that's just selfish; their phones are probably fully charged!

I wind my way around sleeping passengers and eye the outlets in the next gate over. I just need *one* free charger. There's gotta be one that's been overlooked somewhere. Anywhere! Making my way to the gate across from me, I pause. Nora. She's sitting cross-legged by a wall outlet, her eyes fixed on her charging, glowing device, which is resting atop a stack of devices. I hesitate. I guess I *could* ask her if I can borrow it for ten minutes. I don't *think* she'd say no. It's not like she can possibly be mad at me for what happened, and how it all went down, but . . . I'm not exactly thrilled to talk to anyone connected to what just happened. But if it's between my tablet dying and asking Nora . . .

"Excuse me." I clear my throat as I approach her. But her headphones are in. Tentatively, I kneel across from her. Her eyes lift toward me and widen. She lets out a yelp as she pulls out her earbuds.

"Sorry," I say, hushed. "My tablet's about to die. Could I plug mine in for, um, five minutes?"

"Oh. Sure," Nora says, recovering. "But then you have to go back to your parents. My mom said we couldn't get in any more trouble."

She removes her phone and nods to the outlet. I breathe a sigh of relief as I plug in my iPad. Is there anything more satisfying than the buzz when the charger hits the device? Well, probably a ton of things are more satisfying, I guess. But right now, it is everything.

"Some night, huh?" Nora asks me as I settle down next to her.

"I can't believe it really happened," I tell her. "Did you get in a lot of trouble?" I'd seen her mother wagging her finger a lot and frowning, which made me think the answer was yes.

"Sort of. Mostly a lecture about how risky what we did was." Nora rolls her eyes and then looks at me, her expression a bit softer. "And my whole social media implosion . . . People are saying the meanest things . . ." She shudders and then looks at me. "What about you? Everything okay with your folks?"

"It was fine," I tell her. "Just won't be making that mistake again, that's for sure."

"Gonna be hard to make *that* mistake again." Nora laughs a little.

"It's like we were sucked into a video game," I said.

"Or a bad dream?" Nora sighs. She looks down at her phone. "I just—"

But suddenly, my gaze shifts. I straighten. Nora follows my line of sight, then winces and shakes her head.

"Well, great," she mutters.

There's Hanna. Her hands are in her pockets. She's walking purposefully, determined, straight toward Feek. Ruqi is asleep in his lap. He's leaned against the Rube Goldberg machine. Even from here, he looks so tired and down.

"Is she really going to try to get him to help her again?" I ask Nora.

"Oh no." Nora's brow furrows. "That's the one thing my mom promised security. That we'd stay by our parents."

Unbelievable! I *saw* how mad Feek's mother was with him. I didn't need to hear the words to know how they landed on him— the way his shoulders had slumped, his eyes downcast. They *still* look downcast from all the way here where I'm sitting.

I jump up. My heart is racing in my chest, but I'm not going to let that stop me. She's not going to do this. Not again.

"You know how Hanna is," I tell Nora. "She'll talk him into it. We'll *all* get in trouble. They took photocopies of all our parents' driver's licenses!"

Nora stands up too. "Lead the way."

We march toward them. Hanna is talking, but she's too far away to hear. Feek's squinting up at her. And Ruqi—whoa—she is snoring like a jet engine!

Focus, I remind myself. We can't let her rope him in again. But did I mention I hate confrontation? Because I do. I *hate* confrontation. But I think of how Jake yelled at us and kicked us out of the luggage store. The sky lounge and breaking into the locked facility. I remember the look on Feek's mother's face when we approached security. I can't let Feek get in trouble again. And we can't all go to jail! We might already be headed that way when they review the security tape, and then they'll *definitely* send us off if we are out and about again.

As we get near, I say, "Stop."

Hanna looks over at me.

"Sami—" she begins.

"Seriously," I interrupt her before she has a chance to launch into a speech about animal welfare. "Leave him alone. Leave *us* alone!"

Nora backs me up. "This is serious, Hanna. We could get in big trouble. My mom is worried that the press is going to find out about this and try to make it into some huge deal. And, you know, the whole Internet pretty much thinks I'm a liar now."

"How many times did I say this wasn't a good idea?" I exclaim. "But no, you just *had* to get your way. You talked all of us into that mission. It was all your fault!"

Hanna moves to speak, but I put a hand up to stop her. I'm not done yet!

"I know. A cat was in danger. Fine. You're right. But you put *all* of us—human beings—in danger! Do you even care about that? Or do you only care about cats?"

I take a deep breath. I feel a little shaky. What is happening to me? Talking back to my parents. Telling Hanna exactly what I think? But I have to admit, it feels kind of good to say exactly what's on my mind.

But what happens after I finish talking? That doesn't make me feel good at all.

Hanna swallows, tries to speak, but then stuffs her hands in her pockets and stares at the ground.

"Hanna." Feek clears his throat and glances at me and then at her. "Maybe you should go back to your gate. It's just been a long night, we're all a little tired, I think. It's fine."

Hanna looks up at me. Her eyes go glassy, and then—a tear slips down her cheek. Her lower lip trembles. She nods, and then, in a quiet voice, she says, "Yes, this *is* all my fault, Sami."

CHAPTER 41

HANNA

"I'M HERE TO SAY SORRY, SAMI." I SINK DOWN TO THE FLOOR.
"I'm not here to get you to follow me again."

Sami shuffles his feet in response. He looks mortified, but not as mortified as I feel.

"It's cool, Hanna. You don't have to say sorry. I . . . I wanted to find Snickerdoodle." Feek's face looks guilty. "But now, you should go to your dad," he says. Again. "Everyone should go back, I mean."

"I can't go back," I whisper, afraid to look at them. "Everything's my fault because I was trying to run away from my dad."

Everyone's quiet for a moment—except for Ruqi's snoring—and then Nora speaks. "So this isn't about finding a cat?"

I nod my head and then look up at her. "It *is* about that. I want to find Snickerdoodle—I mean, I *need* to find her. But—" I pause. The next part is also the truth, but not one I'm proud about. "I also didn't want to be at the gate with my dad. Because I don't want to talk to him," I finish softly.

Nora eases herself down, and I'm surprised to see her crossing her legs to take a seat on the floor with me and Feek. "Why? Beause he can be as annoying as my mom?"

"Speaking of moms, keep your voices down. If my mom finds out we're doing this again, all your moms will be involved!" Feek hisses, reaching down to stroke Ruqi's head.

"My mom would probably just tell me to go on another"— Sami pauses to use air quotes—" 'adventure.' "

He takes a seat with us and rolls his eyes.

And that does it.

I start crying.

Everything I'd held in this weekend just gushes out into my hands, which made it to my face in time to cover it, to stop the others from seeing all the pain in me that's now turning inside out.

They let me cry in peace, and that lets me slowly calm down until I feel safe enough to lower my hands.

"Are you okay?" Nora asks, her voice gentle.

They're all looking at me: Sami's eyes are scared, Nora's are worried, and Feek's are sad.

"I'm okay." I nod. "I think I'm okay."

Sami shifts. And then, "I'm sorry, Hanna. I didn't mean that *everything* was your fault."

"Yeah." Feek looks at me. "Even if maybe we went too far, it was for a good cause—to help Snickerdoodle."

I gulp and say, "That's not why I'm upset, Feek. I mean, it's not *just* that . . . My dad was trying to find me a new mom at the MONA conference, without telling me."

Sami gasps. "What? How?"

"Are your parents divorced?" Nora asks.

"No, my mom passed away when I was one." I shrug and say the thing I always do to stop people from talking about it too much. "I didn't really know her."

Except it's a lie. I know her. I know her because one of my life missions is to get to know everything about her.

I think I know her more than my brother, Adam, does because I collect facts from everyone who knew her, so I carry many sides of Mom in my brain.

"I'm sorry, Hanna," Feek says, his face matching his words. "How'd you find out what your dad was up to?"

I tell them about using my dad's Facebook account to track Snickerdoodle and then stumbling upon his plans.

Sami looks horrified. "Wow. That's terrible. Trying to find you a new mom."

"Hanna, I'm not trying to be mean," Nora says, "but since you didn't know your mom, is it really that terrible if your dad is trying to find you a new one?" One of Nora's eyes is scrunching as though she's worried that I'm going to yell at her. "Again, I'm not trying to be mean. Just wondering if maybe there's another way to look at this . . ."

I bring my knees up, wrap my arms around them, and rest my chin on top. I look at each of them. Sami, Nora, Feek.

Three kids I met at the airport.

Who I'll probably never see again.

Three kids who tried to help me with one of my missions in life: being there for poor, defenseless animals.

Maybe I can share my other mission with them too.

So they can also understand why Dad can't just replace Mom so easily.

So I tell them about Mom.

The things I hold close, the things I don't want to forget, and even the funny things.

In my investigation of Mom—not missing but gone from this earth, awaiting in another dimension—I learned that she liked to dance but did it so badly, everyone always asked her to stop, but one person never did: Dad.

I learned this fact from Dad.

Adam said the reason *he'd* asked her to stop was because she did this one dance of hers whenever she saw him down the hall at school, the school where she taught and he studied. "Am I upset now that I asked her to stop dancing? Now that she's gone? No, not at all," Adam had said when I'd asked him for more details. "Because I was actually saving her from embarrassing herself."

Then he showed me how she danced. I'd laughed, but later, in my room alone, I'd learned each step of it.

"How did she dance?" Feek interrupts. "It can't be that bad."

"Yeah, show us," Nora says, a smile on her face.

That smile makes me get up. I plant my feet shoulder-width apart and cement them into the ground. Then, from the hip up, I move forward and back, and lift up my arms and lock my elbows at my waist and then swivel my wrists around each other without touching.

"Okay, now *that's* bad," Feek laughs. "Your legs aren't moving."

Sami laughs too, and I sit down and beam at him. *Maybe one day I'll tell him Mom danced like him.*

Nora's still grinning, but she's become quiet.

MY HEART ACHES FOR HANNA. I CAN'T IMAGINE WHAT IT would be like to lose your mom. As much as Mom gets on my nerves sometimes, deep down I know it's because I want more of her. I know it's because she's everything to me.

I've been so absorbed with all my NokNok drama when Hanna has been dealing with so much more. And, to make matters worse, we were so hard on her.

I look at Hanna in her MONA T-shirt and hoodie, and it's like I'm seeing her for the first time.

"I'm so sorry, Hanna," I say. "About what you're going through and for talking about my mom so much."

Hanna swats away my words as if they are bothersome flies. "You don't need to be sorry about that. If my mom was still alive, I'd talk about her all the time too. I know my mom would be someone like Congresswoman Najjar, changing the world."

I'm relieved I didn't offend Hanna, but now I feel dishonest, letting her think that my love for my mom is so pure and uncomplicated when I spent this whole weekend feeling sad and disappointed. Most of the day, I wanted to pull away from her.

I sigh so loudly that it surprises me, and suddenly I'm sharing things I never thought I'd tell these kids. "I am really proud of my mom, but that changing-the-world part is hard. Like, this was supposed to be a special weekend just for us, and we were going to the Chocolate Garden, which is my favorite place in the world, so I was planning all this content around it. But then we got here, and she was so busy at MONA all weekend that by the time we got to the Chocolate Garden, it was closed."

Sami and Hanna both offer sympathetic glances, but I can tell they don't get why this is such a big deal to me. "I know it sounds like I'm whining because I didn't get to go to some candy store, but it's more that my mom is there but we're not really together, if that makes any sense."

There's a long pause, and I'm surprised when Feek says, "I feel that. My dad's gone all the time."

CHAPTER 43

FEEK

DID I REALLY JUST SAY THAT ALOUD?

Then I hear Nora say, "My mom belongs to everyone but me," and it's like someone slaps me upside my head and says, *this is what you've been feeling. This is what you've been knowing. How come you didn't figure this out before now, Feek?*

"Yeah . . ." I rub the back of my head. "Who said everybody else gets to have them?"

Three sets of eyes look back at me confused.

"My dad belongs to everyone else, like your mom. Why do they get to have them?"

"Your dad's a politician too?" Nora asks.

"No, he's an, um . . . lyricist." Explaining my dad's job is tricky. He doesn't call himself a rapper, although he definitely sounds like one. He doesn't call himself a poet, although he definitely sounds like one of those too.

Sami speaks quietly to himself like he's figuring out a math problem, "Lyricist . . . Stiles . . . Like Salaam Stiles? The Muslim Lyricist? Salaam Stiles is your dad?!"

"Who?" Nora asks.

"Yeah—" I say, before being cut off by Hanna and Sami.

"Why didn't you tell us before?!"

"I went to his show!"

"My dad LOVES him!"

"Is he here? In the airport?"

"My brother plays his stuff all the time!"

"We have his book! Would your dad sign it?"

My eyes dart to my gate. Mom's still lying down. Nora and I share a look.

"Shh, remember Ruqi," Nora tells them.

If *thank you* and *you're welcome* can be said with eyes, Nora and I do.

"Sorry I didn't tell you about my dad. Sometimes, it's just easier."

When Hanna and Sami look confused, I explain further.

"People act funny. They forget that public figures and their families are people too. Probably why the Hoffmans are being secretive about who they are."

When everyone leans in and looks at me strangely, I realize my mistake. *Oh no!*

"The Hoffmans? What secret?" Sami asks.

"You know the Hoffmans?" Nora asks.

"Tell us everything you know," Hanna says.

"It . . . I wasn't keeping it from you just to be doing it. The Hoffmans want it a secret. It's obvious." I sigh. No point in hiding it now. "Keep it quiet, please? The Hoffmans are probably Doc and Lala Hoffa."

"No way!" Nora exclaims.

Hanna's eyes bug out.

Now Sami asks, "Who?"

"How do you know?" Hanna asks.

I tell them about the party and the cookie names and even show them the flier with their same floor.

"But I still don't get it," Sami says. "Wouldn't being a celebrity help the cat to be found? Why keep that a secret?"

I try explaining again. "People lose their minds when celebrities are involved. What if people create a ruckus to get Cookie's cat or demand a huge reward? Or worse, sell it? What would the tabloid sites say about her losing her cat in the airport? I don't know Cookie's exact reasons, but it's clear she doesn't want her Lala Hoffa self involved in this."

The other kids nod.

"So, your dad knows Lala Hoffa? I love her! Is your dad here?" Nora asks.

"No, he had to fly right after Fajr for his next show . . . to LA . . . I think LA. Some city with an *L*. All I know is I barely saw him this weekend, and he's not coming home to Philly with us. And I don't know if he's coming back after this show or if he has to go straight to another one."

Hanna is typing fast into her phone. She looks up and says, "He's going to London. He has a few shows there. Then a program with Georgetown University's MSA next week, but nothing for at least a week after that. He'll probably be home then."

I should be happy to learn that, but I feel like I got slapped upside the head again.

"Yeah . . . I guess I should just start googling my dad."

Hanna flushes red and Sami looks away, clearly uncomfortable.

The machine creaks again.

When everyone startles, I say, "It does that sometimes."

I look at my shoes. Creases on the sides. Small and faint, but definitely there.

"He didn't care anyway," I mutter.

"Huh?" Hanna asks.

I'm tempted to change the subject, but Hanna and even Nora have been so real.

"These sneaks," I say. "He likes to wear these kind. So I got them for the conference and kept them perfect. The way he keeps his perfect. But they got messed up from running."

"They still look perfect," Sami says, trying to be nice.

"It's cool. He's too busy to notice."

"I know the feeling. It's *so* not right," Nora says, in the way people do when they're trying to give a hug with their words. Hanna looks like she might actually hug me.

I shake my head. "He's a big deal. How's he supposed to have time for little people?"

"But Feek—" Nora begins.

"Thing is . . ." I cut her and that too-soft voice off again. "He doesn't see I'm not just some little kid anymore, you know? I'll be thirteen in a few months. And I'm getting good at this lyricist thing too. My dad promised to look at my stuff, but he was running late for his flight. But I *know* my dad and I could perform together. I just need a chance."

"A father and son team? That would be cool," Sami says. Nora looks excited too. Hanna looks doubtful.

"My stuff *is* good," I tell her, touching my notebook. "It's not that E-I-E-I-O stuff I did at the sky lounge."

"Could we hear something you wrote?" Hanna asks.

"I mean . . ." I stop when I hear the shaky way my voice sounds. Take a breath. *Look calm.*

"My stuff's good. That's no lie. But I'm working on it. Maybe this morning was a sign. It wasn't worth my dad's time yet. How am I going to share a stage with 'the Salaam Stiles,' saying unfinished lines any kind of way? It's not just my writing. I need to get my performance right too."

Now both Hanna and Nora look doubtful, but Sami . . . His eyes are wide, and he looks like someone just slapped him upside his head too.

CHAPTER 44

SAMI

"IT'S EXHAUSTING TO PERFORM," I BLURT OUT.

Wait. Where did *that* come from? Karate isn't performing! It's a martial art! It's self-defense. It's a sport!

And karate isn't exhausting. Sure, there are times when it gets complicated and I'm stressed about learning a new move, but I love karate. When I'm doing karate, I'm strong. Confident. I'm maneuvering and strategizing and doing my thing.

That's not the kind of performing I'm exhausted by.

"I hate trying to hide my feelings." I say. "And failing. I *hate* being Scaredy-Cat Sami."

"Scaredy-Cat Sami?" Feek repeats. I know he's only repeating what I said, but heat crawls up my neck.

"It's what the kids at school call me." I look at my lap. "It's been my nickname since first grade. When we were little, my brother would tease me too. About how I overthink things and worry about worst-case scenarios. He called me Squir-relly Sami."

"Oh, Sami, that's awful," says Nora.

"It's fine," I say automatically.

Except. I shake my head.

"It's not fine," I say aloud for the first time. "I'm sick of it. Always having to prove I'm not who they think I am when the truth is I *am* who people think I am. I *am* squirrelly. I *do* get scared. I'm always expecting the worst thing to happen. I know it annoys everyone. My parents pretend it doesn't, but I see how they exchange looks. I know what they're thinking."

"If you overthink things, so what?" Nora says. "Your overthinking helped us today."

I frown. "How?"

"Back in the restricted area. You ran through all sorts of different scenarios, didn't you? You helped get Hanna and Ruqi to join us from the storage closet."

"And it was your idea to hide behind the potted plants to figure out our next move undetected," Hanna points out.

"That's right." Feek nods. "There was nothing squirrelly or scaredy-cat about you today. Even if you felt scared while helping, you still helped. You did the brave thing."

No one is laughing at me. No one's telling me to buck up and get on with it. Or practice a breathing technique. They're listening to me. But they've only known me a few hours. They don't know me like the kids in school do. Like Ibrahim. They don't have the fully Sami story.

"I'm always trying to live up to my brother," I tell them. "Everyone always goes on and on about him. Including my parents. I was hoping maybe if they saw me in my first competition, they'd see I wasn't just how they think I am. They'd see there might be other sides to Sami too."

"WHY DON'T YOU JUST TELL YOUR PARENTS YOU DON'T LIKE being seen as something you're not?" I say, looking at Sami's face. "My dad just lets me say whatever I feel."

I don't want anyone to think I'm boasting about Dad, so I quickly add, "But maybe that's because my mom's gone. So he wants to be extra nice."

When I say that part—to make Sami, Feek, and even Nora feel better about their situations—something hits me.

Even though Dad has to be double the parent, he chooses to be double nice instead of double strict.

I never thought of things that way before.

Like right now I'm sitting here with everyone because I sneaked away when Dad fell asleep at our gate. But I sneaked away knowing that even if he woke up and saw me gone, he'd read the text I sent him—*Went to apologize to the other kids for getting them in trouble*—and maybe he'd be a little upset, but not enough to come stalking over to get me. He'd be happy I was doing the right thing.

He'd be reasonable.

He lets me be like he let Mom dance.

And I like that.

Maybe he thought he was being reasonable when he tried to get married at MONA. Maybe he thought I'd be happy if he got a new mom for me.

What Nora asked before comes back to me. *Is it really terrible if your dad is trying to find you a new mom?*

It is terrible.

But Dad doesn't know I feel that way.

I laugh suddenly, breaking the somber mood that everyone's in as we're sitting here thinking of our own problems. "I told you guys to talk to your parents, like it's so easy, but this whole thing started because I didn't want to talk to my dad."

"Why?" Nora asks, leaning forward. "Do you think something will happen if you tell him what you found out? Do you think he'll get mad?"

"No, he'd never get mad." I shake my head adamantly. "He'll just talk about *it*."

"It?" Sami asks, confused, before realization dawns in his eyes. "Ohh . . . you mean, a new mom?"

I nod, afraid to speak, because there it is, sadness bubbling inside again.

"So let's pretend we're your dad. Just say it to us," Feek says.

"Yeah, Hanna. You're looking for this cat all over the airport because you care about her, but what about your own heart?" Nora says. "Imagine it's a little creature too."

I stare at Nora.

My heart. That's the part of me that's hurting the most, that I'd shoved into hiding . . . but who said she, my heart, wanted to be treated like that?

Sami straightens up and sits tall. "I'll be Hanna's dad," he whispers. Then he turns to me and speaks in a deep voice. "Hanna, did you want to talk to me?"

Even though I'm crying, I laugh through the tears and practice sharing my heart with Sami, Feek, and Nora.

I practice and practice, and then I tell Sami it's his turn.

Because he's also shoved his heart aside.

Maybe each one of us has.

But it feels so good to let mine out here in this little space we've made between us. And I want them all to feel the same.

CHAPTER 46

SAMI

"I'M NOT SURE WHAT I'D SAY TO MY PARENTS." I FIDGET. ALL eyes are on me again. "It's not like my parents are wrong. I'm not exactly calm and relaxed."

"I mean, I stay calm and that works for me," says Feek. "But you? Even if you're a little squirrelly, that works for you. So what?"

So what? Feek, with the cool white sneakers and a father who is an honest-to-goodness celebrity, thinks my stressful self is a nonissue? But . . . they've only known me a few hours. They don't know me like people back home do.

"I bet it helps you in karate," adds Hanna. "Don't you have to be on your toes to anticipate your opponent?"

"Oh. I guess that's true," I say slowly. "My karate friends like it when I overplan. Sensei Madea says I'm his right-hand man."

"There you go. Who needs those kids who don't get it?" Feek scoffs. "If they can't see you for how cool you are, it's their loss."

"That's right." Nora nods.

I let these words sink in. It's true they've only known me a few hours. But they've seen my stressed-out side. And they think I'm just fine—great even. Maybe I've been doing it all wrong. Instead of trying to prove to everyone I'm like Ibrahim, maybe I should spend more time accepting myself the way I am. There are people who see me, and they like this version of Sami just fine.

"THAT'S REALLY GREAT THAT YOU HAVE FRIENDS LIKE THAT
in karate, Sami," I say. "I pretty much ruined every friendship I
have this weekend."

Sami frowns. "But how? You've been here all weekend." After
a pause, it dawns on him. "Oh, the whole NokNok thing?"

I shrug and glance at my phone. "It's such a big mess, between
all my NokNok posts about Snickerdoodle and my birthday being
tomorrow—well, I guess it's today, actually."

"Nora, it's your birthday!" Hanna yelps. "Why didn't you tell
us? Happy birthday!"

Feek is quick to bring a finger to his lips, but after he confirms
that Ruqi's sound asleep, Feek and then Sami each whisper their
own birthday wishes.

Feek adds, "Man, we should have been the ones getting you a
Cinna-Yum."

I laugh. "The Cinna-Yum was actually part of my disappointment. I was pity-buying myself a cinnamon roll to make up for
the Chocolate Garden being closed. And I know you guys probably think that my work on NokNok is all for attention, but I
guess some of it's competition. My two best friends passed me

in their follower count, and I got carried away with this whole Snickerdoodle search because it was getting my numbers up. But it all blew up in my face."

"You mean because of everything you posted about Snicker-doodle?" Hanna asks.

"That, and there's something else. Something worse," I say.

I don't want to tell them about Sumaya, but I'm also tired of holding the story in.

Before I can stop myself, it all comes pouring out of me, everything that Sumaya overheard Kennedy, Mackenzie, and me say about her in the bathroom. How I've been messaging with Sumaya since but still told her I wasn't having a birthday party because I thought it would be weird to have her there at the same time with Kennedy and Mackenzie. How she found out I was having a party but didn't invite her. And how my live video made me look like even more of a liar to her.

Nobody says anything, and in that pause, I feel queasy. I can't take the quiet any longer. "I know. It's messed up. I'm messed up."

"You're not messed up, Nora," Feek says. "You just don't know where you belong. Like, now you're here, hanging out with us, so I see you as one of us, Muslim kids, but is that how you see yourself?"

I shrug. "I don't know. Like, how can I be Muslim? My parents don't do any of the prayers I saw you all doing, so I don't know how to do them, and I know you all noticed that I don't exactly dress like I'm Muslim. I saw the way you all looked me up and down when I said I was at MONA."

"But not all Muslims dress the same," Hanna says.

Sami looks embarrassed and lets out an uncomfortable laugh. "Yeah, even I forget that not all Muslims look or dress alike, and I have cousins who don't say their salat or go to the masjid. My mom always says that all Muslim families are different and not everyone practices everything the same way."

I shake my head. I appreciate what Hanna and Sami are trying to say, but deep down, I know this goes beyond appearances. "But I don't even speak Arabic. Like, it's embarrassing how my great-grandparents came from Lebanon, and now none of us remember anything about it. My mom speaks some Arabic, but not enough to teach me. So sometimes I *do* feel like I fit in better with my school friends. It's just easier because I don't have to think about all this stuff that I don't know."

Feek tilts his head to the side. "I don't speak Arabic, and no one in my family speaks Arabic, and that doesn't make me any less Muslim."

Sami says, "Not me either."

Hanna adds, "Nope. I mean, I take Quran lessons and read Arabic, but that's about it."

Now I'm the one who laughs uncomfortably. "Okay, I get it, not all Muslims speak Arabic, but I'm not like you guys. Like I recognized some of you from MONA because you had your pack of friends that you were rolling with, but none of you noticed me because I didn't belong there. Those are your people, not my people. Which is totally fine. It's just that I don't know who my people are anymore."

"Nora," Hanna says, and then she pauses as if she's completely puzzled by what I said. "We didn't know you then, but you're our people now."

Hanna's words warm my heart, and that feeling only grows stronger when she throws an arm around me in a side hug. "I actually totally get it," she adds. "My school friends aren't exactly *my* people either, so I look forward to seeing this crowd all year. When I'm with them, I kind of get tunnel vision to everyone around me, but now you're gonna be in that tunnel with me."

I can't help but laugh. At the start of the day, the last thing I would have wanted was to be in any kind of a tunnel with Hanna, but now it doesn't sound like such a bad place.

But then Hanna pulls her arm away and says, "Nora, you know what, though? I really think you should talk to your friends. Just be honest about what you've been going through. Sumaya will understand, and maybe you'll help Kennedy and Mackenzie think about Muslims differently if they know you're one too. That's pretty much what all of us do. We have to be ourselves and tell people about who we are, and if they don't accept us, we know they weren't our real friends to begin with." She pauses and adds, "I bet your mom also tells you that."

I'm about to say that's exactly the kind of thing Mom would tell me, but a more pressing question comes to mind first.

"So do you guys mix groups at your birthday parties, like you have your Muslim friends and your school friends over at the same time, even if they're not friends with each other?"

Sami looks at me like he doesn't understand why that would be a problem. "Yeah, I've always had birthday parties like that. I used to think it was kind of awkward, but then my brother explained that I have to take the time to introduce everybody and then they'll know each other too." He shrugs. "It works. It makes things less weird."

I'm about to ask everyone if they think I should reschedule my party and invite Sumaya this time, but before I can, the Rube Goldberg machine lets out a loud creak. When we look up, a stray ball is scampering along a metal bicycle chain before it drops to the ground with an unexpected clatter.

AFTER THAT BANG, RUQI'S RHYTHMIC, ROARY SNORES STOP, and I panic. I'm too tired to watch Ruqi right now. When she wriggles, I try rocking her the way Mom does with Hamza. Ruqi lets out a snore, and I let out a breath.

"Wow, you do that just like a dad," Hanna says.

Something about that makes me lose the calm I've been holding on to.

"I'm *not* a dad, though. I'm not. Ruqi has a dad, and he's not me." I bite down on the words to keep myself from shouting. I can't calm this down. I can't! Not when everything in me is screaming.

"Nope! Not a dad. I just get to do the job of Ruqi's dad while still getting grounded like a little kid."

"Sorry, Feek," Hanna whispers.

The looks on her and Nora's and Sami's faces quiet the scream inside.

"No . . . I shouldn't have gotten mad. It's not you. It's . . ." My voice shakes, but I don't try to fix it. "This whole conference, this whole trip—this was supposed to be family time."

"Your dad did the same thing my mom did with me," Nora says in that too-soft voice again. But I don't get mad at it now. I'm too tired to pretend I don't need it.

"Yeah, he promised. He told Mom we'd have family time at MONA, like the old days, when Ruqi was the baby, and Dad wasn't so huge, and he was the one carrying her everywhere. I'd play with Ruqi but I didn't have to watch her, and I'd get to play with my friends and with my dad."

"Adam used to play with me at MONA," Hanna says. "Sometimes I wish I could go back to being three and having my big brother carry me around on his back."

"Ibrahim used to carry me around MONA too!" Sami laughs. "He knew how to do it so it wasn't so scary."

"Yeah?" I wonder if Ruqi will remember me carrying her around. What things will she remember about me at MONA? I push away the image of me yelling at her.

"I gave Adam a hard time too, always running off like Ruqi." Hanna giggles.

"Why am I not surprised?" Nora chimes in, and we all laugh. Then, she says a little sadly, "I wish I had siblings."

"It's nice having a little sister and brother every now and then. It's just . . . it's hard to like it when you have to feel like a dad too."

"This sounds like another Hanna moment," Sami says quietly.

"A what?" Hanna asks.

"It's a 'Why haven't you told your parents? I tell my dad whatever I feel' moment," Sami says, imitating Hanna's way of talking.

We all chuckle at this, even Hanna, who puts her hands on her hips and says, "HEY!"

"So, why don't you tell your dad?" Sami asks.

"What do I say? I'll probably sound like a whiny baby."

"You can't be serious. You're worried about how this will sound to your dad? You told a room full of strangers 'the cat in the hat is not all that' without flinching," Nora deadpans before cracking a smile.

I cover my face and groan but can't help giggling with the others. "You heard that? That line was so, so *baaaad*."

"Yup. I heard it when we were about to leave the bathroom, and I yelled, 'Look, in the sink over there!' to turn that attendant right back around." She covers her mouth to keep from laughing out loud. "But seriously though, you didn't sound like a baby when you told us about your dad." The group nods in agreement.

Hanna chimes in, "Tell him what you told us. You don't like being treated like Ruqi's dad, and you need time with him, and you need time to just be Ruqi's brother."

"Should we practice it?" Sami asks.

"Yes, yes, we should, but *I* get to play Salaam Stiles!" Hanna says.

It looks like Sami is about to vie for the role when the creaking sound from the bottom of the machine comes back, louder than I've heard it all evening. A metal ball drops and bangs, bangs, BANGS into more metal.

We gape at Ruqi, whose eyes have flown open.

YOU WANNA HEAR MY DWEAM? I ME-MEMBER IT. COOKIE CAT in her airport house. In the big, big, big, big, big SHINY house. She like shiny houses. She go tat-a-tat-tat-BANG in her house!

Can I go in her house? I wanna hold her.

I see faces. Scaredy-cat faces. Feek fwiends. My fwiends. Don't be scared, fwiends. This a happy dweam!

Night night come. Black night night. Night night smell like Feek hands. Smell like fwench fwies with extwa ketchup. I want extwa ketchup.

My bed a boat. Rock-a-boat, rock-a-boat, rock-a-boat, rock-a-boat, rock-a-boat . . .

Tat-a-tat-tat-tat-BANG-BANG-BANG!

I move Feek hand. 'Bye, night night. Hi, Feek and fwiends!

There go Snickerdoodle house. I me-member it.

When she look out the door, I yell, "Wait, Snickerdoodle! I wanna hold you!"

I WANNA HOLD YOU!
I hold Ruqi down.
Snickerdoodle, wait!
That banging sound
Her house! Ruqi shouts.
Ruqi, keep it down!
She there! Ruqi points.
So I turn around.
   Wait.
      What?
         WHOA!

            I saw a tail!

         Did you see it?

            I saw a tail too!

         Where?

         There!

A gray and fluffy tail!

Right there!

It's Snickerdoodle. It has to be!

In the machine?

In Snickerdoodle house!

In the panel! There's a crack!

A cat can fit in that?

I wanna hold you!

Shh, speak softly. Don't scare her.

Doodles . . .

Psss, psss, psss . . .

HER FOOT!

Ruqi, don't grab—!

RWAAAAAAAAAAAAAWR! HISSSS!

Blast off, it's a race!

Cat springs into space!

Now we on the chase,

Dash past all the gates!

Snicker's quicker, we can't get her!

Dashing faster! Faster, faster!

Pick up, pick up, pick up!

Pick up the pace!

CHAPTER 51
NORA

WHAT? WOW! SNICKERDOODLE IS HERE, AND MAN, IS SHE A runner. Snickerdoodle bolts out of a loose panel at the base of the machine. Without a word, we take off after her in a repeat of our great race out of the international terminal.

This time, Hanna takes the lead with Sami. Ruqi grabs Feek's neck, and they hitch it piggyback style. I'm bringing up the rear. We charge as fast as we can past one gate and then another. Hanna shakes her bag of kitty treats and loud-whispers, "Snickerdoodle, come here, Snickerdoodle."

Between the sound of our feet pounding the airport linoleum and Hanna's calls, people stir at every gate we pass. Some of them shout:

"Quiet down!"

"People are trying to sleep here."

"Go back to your parents."

Hearing the word *parents* makes me uneasy. I think of my mom's promise to Mr. Rock. They're all going to be so angry when they find out we've taken off again.

A traveler goes up to a gate agent, and I hope he's not asking them to call security. At this rate, we could be grounded in this airport forever. We've got to get to Snickerdoodle before they catch up to us.

"You guys, faster!" I call out.

Sami looks back and waves before charging on. Feek looks back too and catches my eye just as Security Guard White pulls up in a golf cart.

Feek slows down, but I wave him on. "Go," I say. "I've got this."

I start talking before White can. "I know we promised to stay at our gates, but we actually spotted Snickerdoodle this time. You'll help us, won't you? We're so close."

I glance behind me. By now the group is approaching the food court and pointing wildly.

I gesture in their direction. "It looks like Snickerdoodle went in there."

White smiles. "What are you waiting for? Hop in."

I jump in the front seat, and we gun it down the terminal fast enough for the wind to blow through my hair. I feel a shot of excitement, like I'm on a rescue mission in a movie. Snickerdoodle, we're on our way!

CHAPTER 52

HANNA

I TELL EVERYONE TO APPROACH SNICKERDOODLE AS THOUGH she's a rare animal in the jungle. By being gentle and slow with our footfalls, we're able to herd Snickerdoodle into a quieter part of the food court.

Right by Cinna-Yum.

She's a little more relaxed now. I can tell by the way her tail is lifting slightly.

There are fewer people here. It's the perfect place to get her to trust us.

I kneel low to the ground, and everyone follows suit. But they do it so abruptly that Snickerdoodle turns around to look at us and then quickens her pace to get away.

"We can't afford any sudden movements now. We're onto Operation Gain Her Trust," I whisper to the others. They nod, and I appreciate that it's in slow motion and quiet.

I croon, "Snickerdoodle Mildred Hoffman" and shake the salmon treats. Snickerdoodle turns around again tentatively. "It's okay, baby. We love you. We just want to help you."

I open the treats bag and make sure to make a lot of noise doing so.

"Shh," Ruqi whispers to me, still latched onto Feek's back.

"No, this is part of the operation," I explain to Ruqi. "See how she's hesitating? She heard one of her favorite sounds—"

Screeeecch.

A golf cart with Nora and Security Guard White slams its brakes behind us, and Snickerdoodle—who'd completely paused to look at me and her treats—disappears into the grates closing off Cinna-Yum from the world.

IT'S WAY PAST MY BEDTIME, SO IT'S POSSIBLE I'M SLEEPING and this is a dream I'm having on a cot at gate 7, waiting for our flight to come. But it isn't a dream. This is happening. Even if the world feels like it's stopped spinning on its axis. Even if all the noise around me is muffled. We really saw Snickerdoodle. White-and-gray cat. So fluffy. And scared. So scared she zipped between my legs and squeezed through the metal grates of the closed-up Cinna-Yum shop.

"What is going on here?" a sharp voice bellows.

I watch a very real and very nondreamlike man in a gray suit rush toward us from around the corner. I recognize him. He was the smug man who'd told Hanna she misunderstood everything about the animal situation. Who threatened to get us in serious trouble.

"The cat!" Hanna's voice rises. "She went through the grate there." She points. "We have to get her!"

"What on—"

"It's true!" Nora cries out, running toward us. "I saw her too."

"Kids are right, Bruce," B. White says. Her eyes are animated. "Saw her myself."

Bruce looks at the door. He checks his pockets. "Not sure I have a key."

"I got it." White pulls out an enormous key ring. "One of these has got to work."

She tries the first one and shakes her head. Then the second. Is she going to go through *all* those keys? I stare at her. Snickerdoodle could be jumping up to a counter and a fridge and back into the ceiling by the time she figures this out!

I hear a huge clang, followed by what sounds like a million pots falling to a metal surface, and then a meow. A strangled meow. Hanna lets out a gasp. Even Bruce's expression pales a little. There's dead silence now. My heart races. That does not sound good at all.

This *poor* cat. We're trying to help her, but she doesn't understand. She can't see through her fear that everything would be okay if she just took a deep breath and let us help her. If she could stop worrying about all the possible dangers and just take a chance that maybe help was finally at hand, she'd be safe. But it's hard to think clearly when you're so scared.

I know a thing or two about that.

B. White is mumbling. Her face is flushed. She tries another key. Then another.

A frightened meow shrieks from behind the gate. *Is she in danger?* I wonder.

As though reading my mind, Feek nervously says, "She's stuck, isn't she?"

"Or . . . hurt?" Officer White says with a worried expression.

I swallow.

"She could be trapped under a pile of pots." Nora's voice rises. "Or tied up in something."

Hanna's voice wavers. "We have to help her."

She's right. Snickerdoodle needs help.

"One of these has gotta—" White exhales, and then she smiles. "There we go!"

"Finally," Hanna exhales.

We hear a click. We watch as Officer White slides the key out. She pockets the key ring, turns the handle, and then—

"Huh." She pushes the handle and turns it again, but still nothing is happening. Turning to Mr. Rock, she says, "The door isn't budging. I thought Ernie took care of the ones that are sticking."

"Let me try. There's a trick to them." Bruce shoves his arm and shoulder against the door and grunts. It squeaks a little and moves barely a crack. Snickerdoodle cries again.

"Hurry!" Hanna's eyes glisten with tears.

"I'll call Jess." Bruce grabs his walkie-talkie. "She's probably clocked in by now. She's got a way with these."

There's no time to call in people! We need to get in there now. And that's when I realize that I'm the one who can help.

"I got it!" I shout.

Before anyone can react, I sprint full speed toward the door. Beads of sweat form along my forehead. I might open the door. Or I might break my ankle against the hard steel. I run closer and closer, lean back, push out any thoughts, and then, with the strongest roundhouse kick I've ever kicked in my entire life, I slam my foot against the door.

There's a loud groan. The door swings wide. It opened! The door is open!

Everyone hurries forward in a stampede, but Hanna cries out—"Wait! Stop!"

We all pause midstep—even the guards—and look at her.

"Just me," she says. "Please. Give me a chance with her one-on-one."

I expect them to frown. For Bruce to chuckle at Hanna, thinking she can just boss everyone around, but Hanna is standing so still. Her expression is more serious than I've ever seen her—and for some reason, we all grow quiet. We let Hanna make her way past us. She steps inside. I hope she has the right idea.

I hope we aren't too late.

THERE SHE IS. ON THE STAINLESS STEEL COUNTER, RIGHT between the pile of steel bowls and trays that must have fallen over when she jumped up there.

I'm grateful I'm the only one in this room behind the back counter of Cinna-Yum. If everyone else had barged in too, Snickerdoodle would not be staring at me the way she is right now.

It's a mixture of fear and an appeal for help.

It's like my heart—hiding from Dad but needing him too.

I sit down on the ground and cross my legs. I need Snickerdoodle to know she has the upper hand. That she can let me know when she's ready. That I'll listen to her and be patient.

I take out some treats and put them in my palm. "I know you must be so hungry. You need real food, and we'll get you that. But sometimes treats make things better." I speak low and sweet. I continue talking to her, telling her things about her family. How they've been missing her so much. "They're heartbroken, Snickerdoodle. Like you. But when you find each other, all your hearts will be lifted. I promise you."

A tiny head peeks over from the counter. The face on that head looks grumpy, but her eyes are a little less fearful.

I keep talking and lift my upturned hand slowly.

Her tiny nostrils start wiggling up and down. She's smelling her treats.

I risk getting up on one knee. She continues watching me.

Getting up on the other knee, I tell her about our adventure in the airport to find her.

How Feek, Sami, Nora, and I got into lots of trouble for her. "We sacrificed things for you because we wanted you to be safe."

I'm standing now and taking tiny steps closer, my arm outstretched. Then my hand is right across from her chin, and she looks from the treats on my palm to my eyes and back again. I blink a lot to show I trust her and that she should trust me too.

My hand goes under her chin, and she bends her head to grab a treat. She eats it quickly and then takes another one. On the third, I run one finger lightly down from the top of her head to her neck.

And she lets me.

Once all the treats in my hand are gone, I gently place the Meow Mix bag on the counter, open it, and let two more fall out.

When Snickerdoodle goes to eat them, I wait until she's finished and then quickly slide one hand under her belly and the other on top of her, and she's in my arms. For a moment she tenses and struggles, but I'm rubbing her and speaking lovingly to her, crooning her name over and over and letting her settle into my calmly breathing chest.

When she stops moving and stills her head under my chin, I take two steps to the door and ease it slightly open with my hip.

"Nora, get in here!" I whisper loudly. "Get the cameras rolling so the Hoffmans know we found her!"

Snickerdoodle purrs faintly in response.

She's going to be okay, insha'Allah.

And maybe it's because she's calming down right against my heart—my sad, frightened heart—but it makes me feel like I'm going to be okay too.

Feek, with Ruqi on his back, and Sami walk in silently, reverently, behind Nora, who has her phone in her hands.

Ruqi reaches out with fingers wriggling and whispers, "Cookie Cat."

I sidle up to where she's hanging onto Feek's back so Ruqi can reach the top of Snickerdoodle's head.

Ruqi strokes her so gently while softly singing "Cookie Cat" over and over. Snickerdoodle closes her eyes and purrs louder. She really likes Ruqi—who seemed to know about Snickerdoodle all along.

Maybe I can train Ruqi to be my assistant for pet investigations. She's a valuable asset.

Nora suddenly thrusts her phone out and says, "Okay, guys, say cheese!"

Feek, Ruqi, and Sami lean their heads in, and all five of us—six counting Snickerdoodle—take a selfie, smiling, mission complete.

SNICKERDOODLE IS CAREFULLY PLACED IN AN ANIMAL carrier. They close the latch, and B. White carries her away on the back of the golf cart. Her eyes look scared again, and her nervous meowing breaks my heart. I wish I could tell her that even if she doesn't know it yet, and even though this moment feels super scary, amazing things are right around the corner. She's going to be fine. Looking around at everyone—Hanna, Feek, Nora, Ruqi, Betty White, and even Bruce—we're all smiling so much, I'm not sure it's possible for any of us to be grinning any more than we are right now.

"Snickerdoodle's hashtag is trending on NokNok," Nora says. "Everyone is so excited that we found her and got her home safely. Even her veterinarian left us a comment saying thank you!"

"The Animal Allies forum is also blowing up." Hanna looks at her phone and grins.

"Whoa! Hold up! I got a message from them on NokNok too!" Nora says. "And the Hoffmans sent a message. They want an address to send reward money to!"

"No reward needed," Feek says.

We all agree.

"Just glad she's safe," I say.

"But that's not all . . ." Nora's smiling so big. I haven't seen her smile that big since I met her. "Feek, they recognized you! They said they know you!"

Feek's jaw drops. "Whoa."

"You did it, Hanna," I tell her. "You followed all the leads and didn't give up. You went back there and got her to trust you. It worked out perfectly. You really pulled it off."

"*We* did it," she corrects me. "All of us together. I think we make a pretty good team."

"That kick! Sami!" Feek gives me a high five. "Those were some superhero moves right there."

"They really were," Nora agrees. "You were like Clark Kent turning into Superman."

"Officially speaking . . ." Bruce clears his throat. I look over at him, surprised. I'd almost forgotten he was there. "I wouldn't condone playing superheroes at an airport again." But then, with a smile, he adds, "But way to go, kids. That cat looked like she'd had quite an ordeal."

"So that means we're safe, right?" Nora asks. "There's clearly no need for any more investigating everything from earlier today now, is there?"

He's about to respond when a bell chimes through the airport, followed by an announcement. The storm has receded, and flights will be resuming shortly.

When the announcement finishes, Bruce says, "You did us a real service. No more airport antics going forward though, okay?"

"Well, I hope now that we've had this *really* close call"—Hanna straightens and puts a hand to her hip, her fingers dangling inches from her scarf lasso—"Hurston Airport can make sure this never happens again to another innocent creature."

I grin, and Bruce joins me in smiling at Hanna. She is 100 percent back to form.

"You all must be parched," Bruce says. "I can unlock one of these restaurants and get you some pop, lemonade. You name it."

Nerves flutter inside me like a swarm of tiny butterflies because, suddenly, I know exactly what I want, even though it's a big ask. Normally, I'd take those nerves as a sign to stop talking. Fast. But this time, I understand those nerves are just letting me know that things might not go according to plan, and it's okay if they don't. Sometimes there's a lot of great things to find in what doesn't go according to plan.

"Actually, Mr. Bruce." I glance at Nora. "Instead of soda . . . can we visit the Chocolate Garden?"

Nora's eyebrows shoot up.

Bruce looks taken aback. "The Chocolate Garden?"

"It's Nora's birthday," I tell him. "Her thirteenth birthday, actually. She was hoping to check it out while she was in town but didn't get a chance. And this one was closed."

"Ah, that's right." He nods. "It was holiday hours, I think. But . . ." He glances at his watch. "I'm afraid it's not the best time to call Flora to see if I can let you in."

"We won't make a mess," Hanna says quickly.

"Pwease?" Ruqi asks.

"Kids—" he begins.

Normally, I'd just be grateful we aren't going to be arrested or barred from ever flying through Hurston Airport again. I look at Hanna though, and I smile. I turn to Bruce and say, "Sometimes it's better to seek forgiveness than ask permission. Just this once?"

Bruce studies us. He's thinking. Debating. And then—

He walks over and unlocks the door. "Flora won't mind—I'll explain everything to her. Why don't you kids help yourself to some delicious chocolate? It's on me."

"What! Really?" Nora bursts into a smile and claps her hands. "Thank you, thank you so much!"

Bruce flicks the lights on in the store, takes a step back, and waves with a flourish to welcome us inside.

As I step toward the door, I hear my name.

"Sami!"

My parents. They're hurrying toward me, towing their luggage, looking like the dictionary definition of frazzled.

"We were looking all over for you," my father says, catching his breath as he draws close. "Looks like the rain is clearing soon. Plane is on its way from Newark. We should be boarding in an hour or so."

"That's great!" I exclaim.

"And good news." My mother smiles. "Sensei Madea emailed me back and—"

"You emailed him?" I gawp.

"You know, sometimes you have to give your parents a *little* credit." My mother laughs. "I've been trying to figure out how to make this all work ever since we were grounded. We should have enough time to drive you up in time for your competition."

"You'll miss the bus ride," my father says. "I know you worked hard on planning that."

"And we *might* not make it back in time," my mother adds quickly. "There's a lot of moving parts."

"That's okay," I say. "If the competition doesn't work out, it'll be fine."

"Yeah?" my father says. My parents exchange glances.

"Yeah. Sometimes one thing doesn't work out, and something else unexpected might. And even if you can't know it at first, it might end up being something that was exactly right for you and that you needed more. There'll be other competitions."

Bruce walks up to us. "No chocolate for you, buddy?"

"Chocolate?" My mother looks surprised.

"After their heroism, I'd say it's warranted." The security guard puts a hand on my shoulder. "Your son kicked open a stuck door so we could go inside and rescue the missing cat."

"You . . . did?" My father blinks at me.

"Roundhouse kick." I grin.

"I was letting them grab some chocolate as a thank-you," Bruce says.

"Is it okay?" I ask my parents. "I won't be long."

"Go on." My mother smiles. "There's time. Have fun with your friends. Sounds like you've earned it."

A warm feeling glows inside me. I turn and hurry into the store. Chocolate lines the walls, the shelves, everywhere I look— but that's not why I feel this warm sensation lit like a gentle flame inside me.

It's because of the people I see skipping through the aisles. Laughing and exclaiming and holding up chocolate bars and bunny-eared gummies. Nora. Feek. Ruqi. Hanna. The warm feeling is because of them.

My friends.

IF I WASN'T SO EXCITED TO GET INTO THE CHOCOLATE Garden, I would have cried. Hearing Sami ask Mr. Rock to open the Chocolate Garden for my birthday can only mean one thing. Everything these guys said to me is true. They are my people. After this wild and crazy night, I now have three—four if you count Ruqi—new friends. The best birthday gift I could have asked for.

But the next best birthday present is getting ALL THE CHOCOLATE. Crunchy Fluffy Dream Bars, here I come!

Even though it isn't easy to pause before rushing inside, I stop to text my mom.

MOM COME MEET ME AT THE CHOCOLATE GARDEN IN THE FOOD COURT AS FAST AS YOU CAN

I shove my phone into my purse and call out, "Trust me. You've got to pick the Crunchy Fluffy Dream Bar."

Like a magnet, I'm drawn straight to the platform that looks like a giant replica of the Crunchy Fluffy Dream Bar. On a shelf to its side, the bars are stacked in the most magical display of hot-pink wrappers over gold foil. Just the packaging makes my heart sing. "Mr. Rock," I call out. "Don't worry. Only one of these is for me. My mom is coming to pay you for the rest."

I grab three extra bars—one for Mackenzie, one for Kennedy, and one for Sumaya. I'll have to do some serious explaining and apologizing, but this time when I reschedule my party, I'm going to invite all my friends.

Just then I see my mom huffing and puffing into the store, dragging both our carry-ons, her laptop bag, and my backpack. Her eyes are tired and red, and her hair looks disheveled in a way that she never allows her hair to look in public.

Hanna intercepts Mom before I get to her. "We found Snickerdoodle, Congresswoman Najjar. We found her! Now the legislating to keep these animals safe can begin!"

Mom looks at Hanna. Then she looks at me with an even more confused expression.

"We're heroes, Mom," I say, "and we're being rewarded."

She brings a hand up to her chest, like she's too touched for words, and then I do something that is so unlike me but what I think Hanna would do if her mother was standing in front of her. I rush my mom with the biggest hug. As soon as she wraps her arms around me, I want to cry through all the emotions of the day—relief, joy, and sadness—but I push those feelings down and say, "I'm going to need a bit more money for this extra candy."

Mom laughs and kisses the top of my head, and says, "Happy birthday, habibti Nora. You know, there is a verse in the Quran that says, 'Allah is the best of all the planners,' and it looks like an unforgettable birthday was planned for you after all."

Instead of cringing when Mom talks to me as if I'm a regular Muslim girl, this time her words roll straight into me. I don't feel like the faker at MONA anymore. That's my family that Mom's always telling me stories about, my great-grandparents and my grandparents, and there's no reason why their traditions can't belong to me too.

"Yeah," I say, "this day was definitely memorable, but I still want to reschedule my birthday."

"Of course," Mom says. "I told you we were just postponing your party."

"But I don't want to reschedule it right away because I have a new friend I want to invite. Her name is Sumaya."

"Sumaya?" Mom says, her eyebrows raised. I bet she's thinking this MONA weekend was a positive influence on me. If I'm not careful, she'll be taking me to all the Muslim conferences now, trying to get me back in touch with my heritage.

"It has nothing to do with MONA. I was friends with Sumaya before this weekend, but I never told you about her."

"Okay, I didn't say anything about MONA."

"I just don't want you thinking that you did some kind of good thing for me by bringing me here. From now on, no more birthday weekends with conferences."

Mom smiles. "Okay, fair enough." She kisses me on the cheek. "It sounds like maybe our family needs some new legislation. You know, to address birthday weekends and also to regulate your chocolate consumption. That's quite a stack."

"It's not all for me," I say, placing the bars in her hand. "Some of these are for party favors, and some of these are for NokNok. I'm thinking of recording one new candy bar flavor a week. Or should I get enough for two flavors?"

"Nora." Mom says my name as if it's a full sentence and she wants me to fill in the blanks. But I refuse to supply the answer she's looking for.

"It's my job, Mom. How many times do I have to explain this? NokNok is my work. I don't even like these flavors as much as Crunchy Fluffy Dream bars, but I'm going to try them for the sake of my audience."

Zora Neale Hurston Airport

Case Notes – Hanna A. Chen

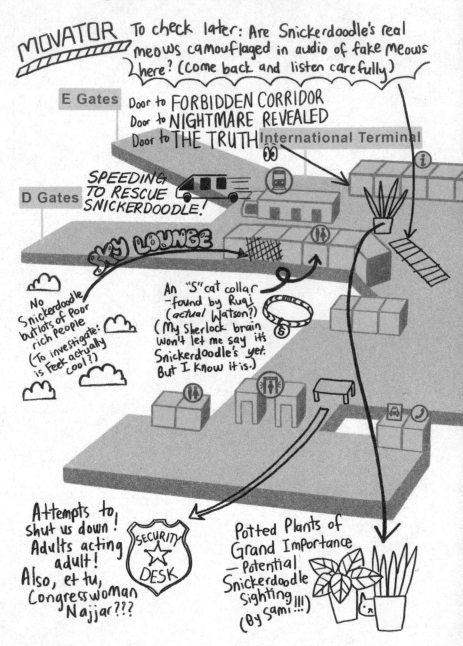

MOVATOR To check later: Are Snickerdoodle's real meows camouflaged in audio of fake meows here? (Come back and listen carefully)

E Gates Door to FORBIDDEN CORRIDOR
Door to NIGHTMARE REVEALED
Door to THE TRUTH International Terminal

SPEEDING TO RESCUE SNICKERDOODLE!

D Gates

SKY LOUNGE

No Snickerdoodle but lots of poor rich people (To investigate: is Feek actually cool?)

An "S" cat collar – found by Ruqi (actual Watson?) (My Sherlock brain won't let me say it's Snickerdoodle's yet. But I know it is.)

Attempts to shut us down! Adults acting adult! Also, et tu, Congresswoman Najjar???

SECURITY DESK

Potted Plants of Grand Importance – Potential Snickerdoodle Sighting!!! (By Sami....!)

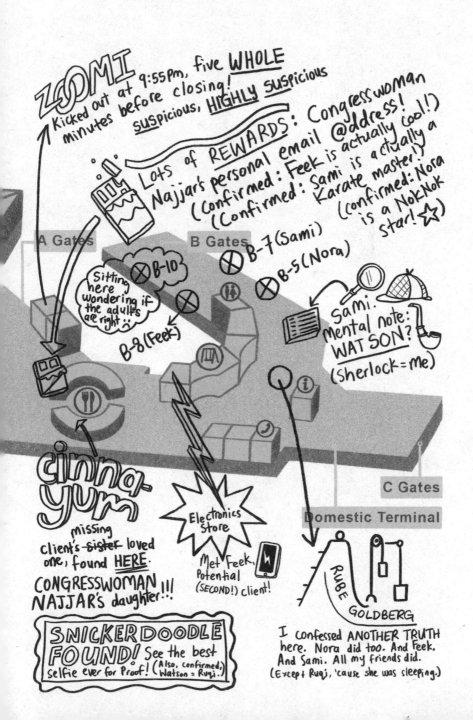

HANNA: Dad! We found her! We found Snickerdoodle!

DAD: Wow, that's amazing but AHEM, I thought you JUST went to apologize to the other kids?

HANNA: I did

DAD: I know. I saw you

HANNA: You did?

DAD: Do you think I was just going to trust your message? I walked over to confirm you were doing the right thing.

HANNA: So you saw us all at the clankity-clang machine?

DAD: Yes

HANNA: THAT'S WHERE SNICKERDOODLE WAS HIDING!

DAD: Really

HANNA: We tracked her down, my friends and me. And I got her to trust us, Dad.

DAD: With that big bag of salmon treats you hid in your luggage all the way from Doha?

I look up from my phone, but not at all the chocolate around me. *He knew I'd come prepared.*

DAD: I know you too well, Hanna

And I know you *too well too, Dad.*

DAD: Where are you now?
HANNA: Mr. Bruce Rock is giving us a reward, but I'll be back soon!

I decide to be kind and not tell Dad, a chocoholic, what the reward was.

CHAPTER 58

FEEK

NOT GONNA LIE—WHEN NORA AND HER MOM HUG AND KISS, I get warm fuzzies inside. And I remember my mom then. I hope she's still asleep. I hope she isn't worried. I hope she understands.

Ruqi tugs my hoodie, interrupting my thoughts.

"We didn't get Nora a birthday gift." Her bottom lip, now stained with chocolate, pokes out.

"We didn't know till late, Ruqi."

"She's our fwiend."

"Yeah . . . yeah, she is."

I watch Ruqi riffle through her pockets. When she doesn't find anything, she touches her unicorn headband, and I know she's thinking about it.

"No, Ruqi! Wait . . . maybe we can do something for her."

"What?"

"We can . . . sing her a song, the birthday song," I suggest.

And before I can say another word, Ruqi grabs Nora's hand and pulls her up on a platform, a giant replica of a Crunchy Fluffy Dream Bar. She belts out at the top of her lungs:

"Happy birthday to yuh! Uh-huh!

Happy birthday to yuh!
Happy BIR-IRTH-day!
HAAAAAA–PEEEEE BIRTH–!"

She's singing the other version. The one Stevie Wonder made for Dr. Martin Luther King. The one Black people sing. She's doing it wrong too. Most people are confused, except Mr. Rock, who is also Black and chuckling. Nora is smiling awkwardly. I have to right this ship. I walk over to them.

"Hey, everybody, we're singing the better birthday song. Clap your hands like this!" I shout.

I get everyone to clap, clap, clap, clap, and once we get a rhythm going, I start singing it.

"Happy birthday to yuh!
Happy birthday to yuh!
Happy bir-irthday!
Happy birthday to yuh!
Happy birthday to yuh!"

And what do you know? People are clapping along and singing with me. I do this part a few times before I say, "Okay, now time to stretch it out!"

"HAAAAAA-PEEEEE BIRTH-DAAAAAY
Ooh yeah!
HAAAAAA-PEEEEE BIRTH-DAAAAAY!"

The thing about this version is it doesn't have a clear ending, so we just keep going and going with this louder birthday song and loud clapping. And as we keep going, others from the airport start to join us. It gets so loud, it's hard to hear me, and Mr. Rock, who has been dancing and singing along, actually hands me his megaphone with a smile. It's five in the morning, and there's got to be at least a few dozen people in the aisles and in the entryway of the store, clapping and singing "Happy Birthday" to Nora. Nora's smile is the widest I've ever seen. She whips out her camera, and when I see Congresswoman Najjar and Hanna also recording, I decide to switch it up.

"Go Nora! It's your birthday! Go Nora! It's your birthday!" I lead the crowd.

To this, she moves from the hip up, forward and back, and swivels her wrists wildly around each other. Too-cool Nora is doing that whacked-out dance Hanna showed us earlier! Hanna and Sami—yes, Sami!—start doing it too. Even Ruqi is trying to do it.

I pause. There's no way to make this dance look cool. None.

But something gets into me. Maybe it's the crowd that keeps growing. I close my eyes and let those wild moves come. I even add a stanky-leg step. I do it smooth.

The crowd roars, and now I hear Nora leading them in a chant. "Go Feek! Go Feek! Go Feek!"

I'm still dancing with my eyes closed when I hear Ruqi exclaim, "I'm his sister! I'm with him! I'm his sister! I'm with him! I'm his sister! I'm with him!"

"Ruqi!" I gasp. "Say it again."

"I'm his sister, I'm with him!" Ruqi jumps up and down. She jumps in front of the rhymes in my head, but I suddenly hear her words aren't ruining them. They're adding to them.

I look out at the crowd, now even bigger. Nora left the platform at some point and is yelling with the crowd, "Go Feek! Go Feek!"

I whisper in Ruqi's ear.

I turn to the crowd. My breath catches in my throat. The megaphone shakes in my hand when I think about what I'm about to do. I think about backing out, but Ruqi looks at me like I'm her hero. Has she always looked at me that way?

I take a breath and shout, "We need a beat, y'all!"

People actually cheer at this, and the way it's so easy to get them to react—the way they've been reacting all along—it makes my *it* happen. The rhymes fall fast and hard. I catch them and throw them out to the crowd.

"It goes a little something like this . . . Boom, bap! Boom, boom, boom, bap!" I point to the crowd, and they repeat me like I knew they would:

"Boom, bap! Boom, boom, boom, bap!"

After we've said it a few times and we have a good flow going, I begin:

"I'm the words to the song
The hammer to the gong
The beats to this rhythm"

"I'm his sister, I'm with him!" Ruqi shouts into the megaphone when I point to her.

"Boom, bap! Boom, boom, boom, bap!"

"She's the rhyme in the line
The music on your mind
The beats to this rhythm
'I'm his sister, I'm with him!'"

"Boom, bap! Boom, boom, boom, bap!"

"We're the bars in this rap
The boom to this bap
The beats to this rhythm
'I'm his sister, I'm with him!'"

"Boom, bap! Boom, boom, boom, bap!"

I end and thank the crowd for their loud applause.

Ruqi is still shouting, "I'm his sister! I'm with him!"

I pull her into a tight hug and whisper in her ear, "And I'm with you. Always with you. Always."

We leave the stage (I mean, the chocolate bar). I return to the ground. To my airport friends, who are squealing. Through the squealing, Nora shouts something about Doc Hoffa liking and resharing a video, but I know I'm not hearing her right, or anything else right, for that matter. I'm stunned speechless now, and the megaphone shakes in my hand again.

And then, I remember. Mom!

"THE BOOM TO THIS BAP
The beats to this rhythm
'I'm his sister, I'm with him!' "

I'm dancing all the way back to gate B10 to Feek's song. Feek *and* Ruqi's song.

I'm dancing Mom's dance, a huge smile on my face as I think about everyone gathered at the Chocolate Garden joining in on the dance too and how Feek made it better with the steps he added. How he made everything come together perfectly—the feelings inside us and the vibes outside too.

I'll never forget Nora's face. It was like bubbles of joy were filling her up, and she had to let them overflow through her eyes and smiles and laughter. Congresswoman Najjar and I recorded it all, and she even gave me a *special* email address where I could send her my video. (And of course I'll be sending her other important appeals from Animal Allies in the future.)

And Sami was so cool, the way he got to be the bravest of all of us just when we needed someone to step up. I'd seriously underestimated him. What a karate kick! And asking to get into the Chocolate Garden!

We all fell into a forever friendship tonight, I just know it. And that feels as good as finding Snickerdoodle.

The Fajr adhan goes off on my phone, and I stop dancing and scramble to turn it off.

It's the only alarm I always have active because I'm usually at home at Fajr.

I unknot the hijab from my belt clip and pull it through slowly, thinking of talking to Dad about MONA. Like I practiced by the Rube Goldberg machine, with Sami, Nora, and Feek.

No, it's not MONA that I have to talk to Dad about.

It's moms. The mom I had before—the one I still have in my heart and will have forever—and . . . the new one Dad's thinking about.

I look ahead and I can't believe it.

Dad is sitting there with a huge smile on his face, staring at me.

Not upset, not impatient, not stern, the way he'd been before he fell asleep.

And not no-nonsense like in his texts when I was at the Chocolate Garden.

He wasn't even just his normal content-Dad self.

Happy. Hugely happy.

Is he hugely happy with me?

"How is it that you're dancing just like Mom used to?" Dad's full-blown laughing now as I get to our chairs. "It must be in the genes!"

I smile back at Dad, and my shoulders let go of the scrunching up they'd started to do. "A long time ago, Adam showed me Mom's dance, and I practiced it in my room until I got it right." I demonstrate the original Mom dance. And then I add the foot movements Feek thought up. "And my friend Feek showed the world how to make it even better. Like this."

Dad opens his arms wide, and I fall into him.

And it feels like *all of me* has permission to finally unscrunch after a whole weekend.

His arms tight around me, Dad whispers, "I'm proud of you for apologizing to the other kids. And for letting me know where you went. And for finding Snickerdoodle. But you're still grounded, Hanna Amelia Chen."

I sigh heavily and roll my eyes above his shoulder. "The airport *thanked* us, Dad. It's going to be all over the media. Can't I get a break for *that*?"

"Before you begin negotiating, let's go pray Fajr." He lets go of me, and I wrap the scarf around my head.

On the way to the bathrooms to make wudu, I tell Dad more details about the Snickerdoodle rescue mission.

It's not to get me ungrounded that I tell him.

It's to tell him that we all worked together, Feek, Sami, Nora, and me. That I didn't need to do my mission on my own.

They were all there for Snickerdoodle.

After Fajr, after dhikr and dua, I reach out to Dad's arm.

"Dad, I was mad at you the whole weekend."

"I know, Hanna."

"It's because of that matrimonial thing you were doing at MONA. I saw it when I used your Facebook account to talk to the Hoffmans about Snickerdoodle." I lower my head and stare at my knees, still in tashahhud pose. "I didn't like that you were trying to get a new mom for me without telling me anything about it."

Dad doesn't say anything for a long time. Then he clears his throat. "I figured you knew. That's why I've been trying talk to you these past few days. But"—he pauses—"I wasn't trying to get you a new mom, Hanna."

"That's what *matrimonial* means. I looked it up." I pull my phone out to show him, but he puts his hand up like a stop sign.

His face is splotchy with red parts. He's embarrassed—*like me. Is it hard for him to talk about it too?*

"Yes, if I got married again, it means you would probably have a mother figure in your life again. But, Hanna, you'd only have one mom, the one who handed down that dance." Dad laughs, and then his voice suddenly breaks a little and he's talking through a sob. "I'd never try to replace Mom for you, ever. She's your mom forever."

"But how come you hid the matrimonial thing from me then?" I'm talking through a sob too. And it hurts a lot.

"Because I didn't want to tell you about something that may not work out. I was afraid of telling you that parents can feel lonely if they've been with a partner before and now they're all on their own, and sometimes we explore how to find another partner who will be good to our kids too. If I told you all that and then went to the matrimonial events at MONA and didn't find a good partner for me, for our family, then I was afraid you might get disappointed." Dad reaches for my hand, and I let him take it. "I want only the best for you. And I guess in trying to save your feelings, I made it all worse. I'm sorry, Hanna."

He whispers the last part, and I lean into his side, our hands clasped, and stare at the black vinyl travel prayer mat we just shared. "I'm sorry too, Dad. For thinking you'd replace Mom just like that," I say.

We sit together for a moment, and then I lift my head from his shoulder and twist to get my backpack that's resting on the floor beside the prayer mat. I was going to save the treat inside for the flight, but maybe now's the best time.

I thrust my hand in and hold out a jumbo, one hundred grams, Crispy Caramel Toffeelicious Twirl Bar.

As he reaches for it, Dad's eyes light up like he's a little kid. Which makes me crack out in a big smile.

He's happy. And I'm happy. Like it's always been between us, until this matrimonial thing happened. Until I tried to run away and hide, like Snickerdoodle, thinking things were better if I didn't face reality.

But, even though running away helped me find Snickerdoodle *and* new friends, things hadn't felt better *inside* me.

I'm glad I ran back—I mean, danced *back—to Dad.*

Giddy, I take a deep breath and just let the question explode out of me, the one that storms my head every time I think about all this. "So *who* exactly is the *partner* you found at MONA?"

And can I approve her??? my brain screams.

"There isn't anyone, Hanna," Dad says, already unwrapping the chocolate bar eagerly. "I promise you that if I get close to thinking, *this is a good partner person*, I'll make sure to tell you."

"Can I help to vote her off if she's not the right one?"

"Absolutely not." He takes a bite of the Crispy Caramel Toffee-licious Twirl Bar and closes his eyes, savoring it.

I tip my head and narrow *my* eyes. "But what if she doesn't like animals? And is like Cruella de Vil and makes coats out of dalmatian puppies?"

"And do you really believe I would say, 'Ah, this is a good partner!' about someone like that?"

"But what if you don't know?"

"When the time comes, insha'Allah, we'll do our research," Dad assures me, wrapping the chocolate bar up. "We'll share the rest of the chocolate on the flight. While we talk about this topic more."

"Aha, you said WE'LL do our research!" I sit up, pleased, my heart lifting with hope.

I can help with the investigation of the partner person. Dad won't even need to hire me. I'll do it pro bono.

Because the client will be him *and* me.

Because, of course, I'd need to thoroughly vet any "mother figure" that comes into my life.

They'd need CIA-level clearance.

"Yes, *we*. That's what we are, a WE." Dad lifts up a hand for a high five, and I grant him one. "But you're still grounded. For breaking rules at the airport and also—thanks for reminding me about this, by the way—for peeking into my private Facebook account."

I groan, but then Dad pulls out his phone and shows me something that makes my heart dance.

He'd sent the heartbroken Hoffmans a message: *I'm so happy Snickerdoodle was found. And I'm also happy that my daughter and her friends found her. Happy reunion!*

I hug Dad for a long time to say thank you. For the message. For talking to me.

And for being so kind.

As Dad folds up the prayer mat, I pull off my hijab and catch a glimpse of my reflection in the glass of a perfume store.

In my MONA T-shirt and my hijab around my neck, I'm looking at a girl who solved a case with her friends.

Who saved a living being.

Two living beings, actually: Snickerdoodle and my heart.

I'm looking at a girl who accomplished two missions.

With another investigation to come: Dad's potential partner person.

I can't wait to open the file on that case.

CHAPTER 60

FEEK

I TAKE RUQI TO THE FAMILY RESTROOM TO MAKE THE LIE I'M about to tell Mom (if she's awake) at least partly true. I make wudu at the sink. (Fajr time is in, and I'm going to need to pray for forgiveness.) When Ruqi comes out of the stall, I see her eyes are droopy.

"Don't worry. We'll get back to sleep soon," I tell her.

We walk past the Rube Goldberg machine, and I look for the opening in the panel, so unnoticeable if you're not looking for it. I see the lever on the machine, and I can't help it this time. I pull it. The pendulum balls start swinging back and forth! Clack . . . clack . . . clack . . . clack . . . clack. Ruqi and I squeal when, like magic, the gears inside start moving and the Rube Goldberg comes alive again. I scoop up Ruqi's winter coat, throw it over my shoulder, and head over to Mom. Ruqi's usual dance walk is now a drowsy sway.

As we near gate B8, I hear an announcement that the flight to Orlando is now boarding. I look across to where Sami is standing with his parents, and even from across the way, we lock eyes and I can tell he's ecstatic. I cup my hands and raise them dramatically to show him I'm praying for him and then do my poor impression of a karate kick. He raises his cupped hands back at me. I can't wait to hear how his tournament goes.

We enter the gate, and I see Mom sitting on my chair with a sleeping Hamza on her shoulder. Uh-oh.

"Hi, Mommy," Ruqi slurs drowsily.

"I, uh . . . Ruqi had to go to the bathroom," I say.

She smiles strangely at me but says, "I thought so. Hamza woke up, but now he's rocked out again."

"Ruqi's about to be knocked out too."

"She's got to be exhausted. Thank you for taking care of her." Mom gives me that strange smile again, then kisses Ruqi's forehead and lays her down.

"Hopefully, she doesn't snore again," I say.

We exchange tired glances.

"It's time to pray. I have to make wudu," she tells me.

"Yeah, I just did mine. Go ahead. I got Ruqi."

"You're really growing up," she says as she straps Hamza into the baby carrier. It looks like she might actually cry. What is going on?

After waiting awhile for her to come back from the bathroom, I remember to take out my notebook and try to recapture the lines that flowed so easily from me on that platform.

"We're the bars in this rap . . ." I'm whispering when Mom hands me her phone. I was so focused I didn't see her return.

"This might help," she says.

I almost fall over. The volume is muted, but I see myself and Ruqi on the screen, dancing on a giant candy bar stage.

"Like I said, Hamza woke up, so I went for a walk. The noise in the food court got my attention. People were yelling your name."

"Mom, I'm—"

"No, no. Don't apologize. I admit, when I saw you two, I was about to march right up there and drag you both off that stage. But then I *saw* you two. Saw what you were doing. I—" Her voice cracks, and she pulls me into a hug.

She says into my ear, "You were brilliant, Feek. Brilliant! And the way you were caring for your sister—"

"Mom—"

"I'm not finished," she says, pulling back. "Something about what you did made me see things more clearly, made me see the truth about this whole weekend. It's been hard on me, but I haven't really thought about how it's been hard on you, how much you've been giving."

"We needed more help, Mom. He promised we'd be together. 'A family vacation, like old times.' He promised," I spit out more harshly than I mean to.

She looks away from me. "Feek . . . let's not talk bad about your dad . . ."

I'm about to drop it for her sake, but I look across and see Hanna talking to her dad as they get ready to board. She waves, and I realize this is a Hanna moment.

"Maybe we shouldn't talk about him, but can we talk *to* him?"

Mom raises her eyebrows. She nibbles her lip, deciding what to tell me. Finally, she says, "The truth is . . . I have talked to him.

Over and over again. Maybe it's time it came from you. Text him after salat. Get the conversation started."

She hands me my phone, and I see that I have a text message from Nora:

Leaving now but thank you Feek!!!! The birthday song! The dance! That rap! SO AMAZING! Best birthday ever! Give Ruqi a huge hug for me. Salaam.

I'm about to text her back when another text pops up from Dad:

FEEKNESS!!! Your mom sent me your video and SUBHANALLAH! We have got to talk about performing together soon!

Dad texts again:

And Doc Hoffa is blowing up my phone. I have no clue how he saw your video! Says he wants to meet you. Not in a big party like last time, but really meet you. Maybe I can tag along?

Performing with Dad? Meeting Doc Hoffa! That excitement I felt onstage comes over me again but dims when I look over at Mom, who is looking at me curiously, and Ruqi, who is fast asleep. What do I say to Dad? This is what I wanted. Why don't I know what to say?

"We need to pray," Mom reminds me.

We stand up in a corner, and I move to Mom's right and wait for her to begin.

Mom shakes her head and says, "Feek, you're getting older. I think it's time you start leading prayer now."

So I do. And as I bow my head on the gray airport carpet, this strange day and this stranger night washes over me. I think about losing Ruqi and then finding her and new friends. Hanna, Sami, and Nora. I think about how we all needed one another. How we all impacted one another in some way. Like metal balls finding their path together and making something magical in a machine.

And I remember being on that stage and the best part: sharing it with Ruqi. And I remember Mom. Our talk settles over me, warms me. And, yeah, I even remember Dad. I miss him. I miss all the great times we used to have.

I thank Allah. I am so, so grateful. Grateful for the people in my life. Grateful because they make me see what's most important. People. They matter most.

With my head still on the ground, I whisper, "Give me the right words to say to Dad."

When we salaam out of the prayer, I know exactly what I'll text back:

Thank you, Dad, but I don't want us to perform. Not yet. I want you home first. We miss you.

Come home.

Because we need each other.

We all do.

SAMI: I'm boarded! Plane takes off in ten minutes.

FEEK: Be safe! Bring home that championship!

NORA: Boarded too. We'll be cheering for you, Sami! Insha'Allah all goes well!

HANNA: Let us know when you've won, Sami!

HANNA: · · ·

FEEK: Guess what? We're not the only ones headed to Philly!

NORA: Wait! Do you mean . . . ?

HANNA: · · ·

FEEK: Dad's coming home! He called me back right after I texted him. I think he was crying. He canceled his shows for us to have an emergency family meeting.

SAMI: That's great! If you need to talk strategy let me know!

HANNA: · · ·

NORA: So happy for you. You got this.

HANNA: GUYS WE HAVE ANOTHER CASE!!! ANIMAL ALLIES—BRUSSELS BRANCH—JUST REPORTED A MISSING CHINCHILLA AT THE AIRPORT!!! SINCE WE'VE DONE THIS BEFORE, WE ARE THE ONLY ONES WHO CAN FIND SIR WILLOUGHBY (THAT'S HIS PRECIOUS NAME)!! WHO'S IN???

HANNA: And that's GREAT Feek!

HANNA: WHO'S COMING TO BRUSSELS? (I'm talking to my dad about making a stop!)

NORA: Hanna . . .

SAMI: • • •

FEEK: Airplane mode! Sorry! Got to go!

ACKNOWLEDGMENTS

Working together on this book has been filled with all the sweetness in the Chocolate Garden, and we'd like to share a special treat with everyone who has been there for us along the way.

A Super-Duper Grand Delight bar to Aisha Saeed, who brought us together with her idea for this joyful confection of a story that has truly redefined the creative experience for us all.

The original Crunchy Fluffy Dream Bar to our incredible publishing team: Erica Finkel, Emily Daluga, Andrew Smith, Jenny Choy, Mary Marolla, Maggie Lehrman, and everyone at Abrams. And to our agents: Essie White, Faye Bender, Paige Terlip, and Sara Crowe.

A Caramel Crunch Dreamsicle from Aisha to her family: Thank you to my husband and boys for reading *Grounded* in its earliest iterations and for your support and love always. Thank you also to my parents for your love and duas.

A Deluxe Toffee Nutty Bar from Huda to her husband, children, and mother for cheering her along at every step of this project. An extra Milk Chocolate Caramel Cookie Bar to her youngest son and for her forever writing partners, Laura and Jennifer, who read early chapters and drafts. And an endless supply of latte-flavored hard candies in memory of Huda's father, Murtadha Al-Marashi.

Jamilah sends Velvet Love chocolate bars with extra-sweet, extra-stretchy caramel to her husband and their boys for their patience, sweetness, and stretchiness from the beginning to the end of this book-making process. Thank you, beloveds, for the random beta reads, the whispered "let's give Mom time to work" moments, and the celebratory dinners during each milestone of this book. A Hugs and Giggles chocolate bar with peanuts and nougat to author Ashley Franklin, who gives Jamilah endless nutty things to laugh about and also gives a hug with words when needed. Jamilah offers chocolate nuggets to KidLit in Color and Black Creators HQ for the constant nuggets of advice and support. Jamilah thanks Black Muslim lyricists/poets/rappers for sharing their Original Extra Rich Chocolate bars with her and inspiring the character of Feek. From The Last Poets who laid the groundwork to the many today who continue the tradition, may the richness of their artistry be honored, even if in a small way, by Feek's story.

From Sajidah, a jumbo Crispy Caramel Toffeelicious Twirl Bar to her three children, two cats, and one husband, in gratitude for being there through all her projects. Also, a cascade of Toffeelicious candies to all the *Love from A to Z* readers who asked for a story for Hanna Chen. Here it is, and in true sibling fairness fashion, like her brother, Adam, Hanna gets to meet people in an airport too!

And to our readers, the Chocolate Garden Variety Box, with one of every flavor. We hope you find the one you love.

AUTHOR BIOS

Aisha Saeed is an award-winning and *New York Times* bestselling author of books for children. Her middle-grade novel *Amal Unbound* received multiple starred reviews and was a Global Read Aloud for 2018. Her picture book, *Bilal Cooks Daal,* received an APALA honor, and she was the coeditor of the critically acclaimed *Once Upon an Eid.* Aisha is also a founding member of the nonprofit We Need Diverse Books™. She lives in Atlanta, Georgia, with her family.

Huda Al-Marashi is the author of the bestselling memoir *First Comes Marriage: My Not-So-Typical American Love Story.* Her other writing has appeared in various anthologies and news outlets, such as the *New York Times*, the *Washington Post*, the *Los Angeles Times*, and al Jazeera. She is currently a fellow with the Highlights Foundation Muslim Storytellers program, and *Grounded* is her first novel for young readers. She lives in San Diego, California, with her family.

Jamilah Thompkins-Bigelow is a Philadelphia-based bestselling children's book author. Her books, which center Black and Muslim kids, have been recognized by many, including *TIME* and NPR, and she is an Irma Black Award silver medalist. A former teacher and forever educator at heart, she is probably most proud that her picture book *Your Name Is a Song* was named the December 2021 NEA Read Across America book and that it is included in the curricula of major school districts throughout the United States.

S.K. Ali is the *New York Times* bestselling and award-winning author of several books, including the Morris Award finalist *Saints and Misfits* and *Love from A to Z*, both named as top ten YA titles of the year by various media, including *Entertainment Weekly* and *Kirkus Reviews*. Her newest novel, *Misfit in Love*, is a *People* magazine best book of summer 2021. Her other titles include the critically acclaimed middle-grade anthology *Once Upon an Eid* and the *New York Times* bestselling picture book *The Proudest Blue*.